THE HEART MODEL™

A New Pathway to Forgiveness for Couples

MATT WADE, LMFT

For permission requests, contact:
Unstuck Therapy, LLC
www.unstucktherapy.org

Printed in the United States of America.

ISBN: 979-8-218-87928-0

The HEART Model™ is a trademark of Matt Wade, LMFT.

DEDICATION

For the couples I've sat with—
your stories, your tears, your attempts to reach for
each other again are the reason this book exists.
You created this work.
I just wrote it down.

CONTENTS

INTRODUCTION

What if forgiveness is less a one-time decision and more a practice — a way of relating to hurt, to ourselves, and to each other over time?

Decades of forgiveness research consistently **show** that people don't simply "decide" once and never revisit it; they move through waves of emotion, meaning-making, and re-opening, often returning to the work again and again as the pain resurfaces in new ways. Real forgiveness is **decided over time, not just declared once and for all.**

What do I mean by "decided, not declared"?

Forgiveness *does* involve a decision — but it's a decision you revisit. It's not a single moment where you say, "It's fine," and never feel anything about it again. Forgiveness is not a linear event; it's a cyclical process, much like healing in all areas of life.

We move through emotions, insights, and conversations toward a deeper completion of the forgiveness process. And as we practice forgiving, we often find ourselves moving closer to reconciliation — when it's safe and wise to do so — or at the very least, toward a more settled, spacious place in our own hearts.

Real forgiveness is decided over time, not declared once and for all.

Every relationship, no matter how loving or steady, eventually bumps into moments that feel too sharp, too confusing, or too heavy to simply shake off.

A comment lands harder than expected.
A promise goes unfulfilled.
A need goes unheard.
A tone feels colder than it should.
A deep marital injury occurs – sometimes many.

A moment that could've brought you together somehow leaves you feeling misunderstood or alone.

You don't have to be in crisis for hurt to happen.
You only have to be human.

Amber and I know this firsthand. Over more than twenty years of marriage, we've had seasons where forgiveness felt simple and natural… and seasons where it felt impossible. There were stretches when we were playful and connected, and stretches when we were just two exhausted people passing each other in the hallway, both quietly wondering, *"Are we okay?"*

We've hurt each other in ways we never intended. We've said things we wish we could take back. We've gone to bed turned away from each other, not because we stopped loving each other, but because we didn't yet know how to find our way back.

What has saved us has never been perfection. It's been repair. Again and again, we've had to practice naming the hurt, staying open to each other's experience, taking responsibility, loosening resentment, and turning back toward each other when it would have been easier to shut down. The HEART Model™ grew out of that lived reality — my work with couples, yes, but also the ongoing, imperfect forgiveness story inside my own marriage.

People often imagine that good relationships avoid pain, but the truth is far more generous: good relationships repair pain. Strong relationships aren't defined by the absence of hurt, but by the presence of repair.

Strong relationships aren't defined by the absence of hurt, but by the presence of repair.

Love doesn't prevent misunderstandings or emotional injuries; love gives us the courage and capacity to work through them.

But here's the tension couples face over and over again: we were never taught *how* to forgive.

Most of us grew up learning how to "let it go," "move on quickly," "stay quiet to keep the peace," or "not make it a big deal." Others learned the opposite — to protest louder, push harder, or demand resolution before either person is regulated enough to offer it.

Both are survival strategies.
Neither leads to healing.

When we don't know how to repair emotional pain, we fall into patterns that feel strangely familiar:

- ⮑ We minimize the hurt so we don't rock the boat.
- ⮑ We ignore it, hoping time will take care of it.
- ⮑ We stuff it, telling ourselves it's not worth bringing up.
- ⮑ We bypass it with "it's fine."
- ⮑ We keep score and build resentment.
- ⮑ Or we explode, because the hurt finally has nowhere left to hide.

And here's the truth: unrepaired hurt doesn't disappear, it accumulates.

Unrepaired hurt doesn't disappear; it accumulates.

It buries itself under everyday life until it shapes how we interpret our partner's tone, intention, stress, silence, or absence. Unhealed hurt becomes the lens through which we see everything — even the moments that were never meant to wound us.

Hurt that isn't honored slowly erodes emotional safety. And safety is the foundation of connection.

Without safety, intimacy becomes effortful.
Distance becomes easier.
Resentment becomes louder and forgiveness becomes harder.

The real work of healing a relationship begins not when everything is calm, but when something has broken your sense of security and closeness — and you decide to turn toward repair instead of away.

But here's where most couples quietly struggle: "I want to heal… I just don't know where to begin."

Forgiveness feels foggy.
Repair feels overwhelming.
The steps feel unclear.
The emotions feel too big.
The stakes feel too high.

And the pressure to "fix it fast" makes everything worse.

This isn't because couples are broken.
It's because they are overwhelmed and under-resourced.

Trying to repair with no map.
Trying to forgive with no process.
Trying to reconnect without understanding the emotional forces pulling them apart.

Unforgiveness — the unresolved mixture of resentment, rumination, anger, and emotional constriction — doesn't just affect the heart metaphorically. It affects the entire body.

Anne Lamott once wrote, *"Not forgiving is like drinking rat poison and then waiting for the rat to die."*

It's a striking image because it reflects what science has been saying for years: the person most harmed by ongoing unforgiveness is the one holding it.

For decades, researchers have found that unforgiveness behaves like a chronic stress response. Studies show it is linked to:

- higher blood pressure
- elevated heart rate
- increased muscle tension
- disrupted sleep
- fatigue and somatic symptoms
- poorer immune functioning
- greater overall health decline

In longitudinal research, unforgiveness has even predicted higher mortality risk in older adults. Among cancer survivors, forgiveness-focused interventions have been shown to increase hope, reduce distress, and improve quality of life.

Forgiveness, it turns out, is not just an emotional idea — it is a physiological intervention, shifting the nervous system from threat to safety.

And yet, almost all of this work on forgiveness has focused on individuals, not on couples.

Why a New Model for Couples?

Forgiveness has been written about for centuries, but almost exclusively as an individual process — an internal journey of letting go, releasing bitterness, or finding closure.

Beautiful work, meaningful work… but incomplete for couples.

In relationships, hurt is not just *internal*.
It's *interpersonal*.

The injury happens between two people.
So the healing must happen between them as well.

What I found in my work with couples — and in my own marriage — is that traditional forgiveness language often falls short. It can feel too individual, too spiritualized, too detached from the real emotional process couples must walk through together.

Couples needed something different:

- ➲ Couples needed a model that was simple.
- ➲ Couples needed a model that was relational.
- ➲ Couples needed a model that didn't rush them toward forgiveness.
- ➲ Couples needed a model that honored both partners' experiences.
- ➲ Couples needed a path back to each other that felt safe, gentle, and doable.

Nearly every major forgiveness model in psychology — Enright's process model, Worthington's REACH, McCullough's meaning-making research — focuses on the internal work of one person.

But healing in relationships is different. It happens between two people who are sharing hurt, history, and nervous systems that are responding to each other in real time.

This is where forgiveness takes on a relational shape — one you can't walk alone.

The HEART Model™ was born from sitting with couples in moments of pain, rupture, courage, and repair. It emerged as a five-step rhythm that felt natural, human, and emotionally accessible — something any couple could practice without needing specialized training or therapeutic language.

HEART doesn't promise quick fixes.
It doesn't demand forgiveness.
It doesn't minimize pain.

Instead, it offers something far more honest: a way forward — toward forgiveness.

A sequence that allows each partner's truth to be heard, understood, honored, and held with care. A process that softens the nervous system, deepens emotional connection, and builds the trust needed for repair.

This isn't just a model for forgiveness. It's a model for **reconnection** — a model for finding your way back to each other when life gets messy and love feels stretched thin.

Couples deserve a map.
HEART is the one I've seen couples help create, shape, and live out in real time.

It's the map they trusted me to witness.
And now, it's in your hands too.

Jordan & Sam

Jordan and Sam had been circling the same unresolved hurt for months.

It began with a moment that seemed small at first — a broken promise, made sincerely but forgotten in the rush of a busy week. Jordan had trusted Sam to follow through. Sam genuinely meant to. But when the moment came, Sam slipped.

And Jordan felt alone.

Not devastated.
Not betrayed.
Just quietly, deeply hurt.

At first, Jordan said nothing. They told themself it wasn't worth making a big deal out of. But the hurt settled in — tight, quiet, persistent. Over time, the story in Jordan's mind shifted:

"Maybe I don't matter as much as I thought."

Sam noticed the distance but didn't know its source. Sam asked if Jordan was okay, but Jordan brushed it off. The silence grew. Both felt the space widening.

Weeks later, on a tense evening, Jordan finally named what had happened — how important that promise had been, how forgotten they felt, and how the moment touched old, unhealed places in their story.

Sam's heart dropped.

They hadn't realized.
They hadn't seen.
They hadn't understood the impact.

And that's where their real story of forgiveness began.

Not with an apology.
Not with defensiveness.
But with presence.

Sam listened — truly listened — for the first time since the moment had happened. They didn't explain. They didn't justify. They simply held the truth of Jordan's hurt with steadiness.

Something opened — the kind of softening that happens when pain is finally seen.

Clarity.
Connection.
A quiet sense of, "Oh… this matters."

When Sam finally spoke, their voice was gentle: "I see now how that moment landed for you. I'm sorry for the hurt I caused. I didn't understand the weight of it, but I do now."

Jordan's body responded before their words did — the breath easing, the jaw loosening, the shoulders dropping. Their nervous system registered the shift before their mind caught up.

Empathy.
Understanding.
Presence.

The beginning of repair.

Forgiveness didn't happen instantly. But the grip of resentment began to loosen because the hurt had finally been held with care. The old story — "I don't matter" — slowly began to dissolve.

In its place, a deeper truth emerged: *I was hurt… and they see me.*

This was the moment forgiveness became possible.

This is the kind of moment the HEART Model™ was built for — not as a theory, but as a lived rhythm. A gentle, structured process couples can follow when pain, misunderstanding, or emotional injuries threaten connection.

What HEART Honors

HEART honors:

➲ your experience

➲ your partner's experience

➲ your nervous systems

➲ your emotional patterns

➲ your attachment histories

➲ your longing for safety and closeness

HEART isn't about perfection.
It's about presence.

It's about curiosity.
It's about having a map when the emotional terrain feels impossible to navigate.

HEART gives you language where you used to have silence.
Steps when you used to feel lost.
Hope when you used to feel stuck.

You don't have to know how to do all of it right now.
You just need willingness.

Willingness is enough.

Because here's what I've learned in every therapy room, lecture hall, and marriage intensive: Most couples are not broken — they're simply overwhelmed, overburdened, and under-resourced.

When couples are given a clear, compassionate framework, they soften faster.
They understand each other more deeply.
They take responsibility with more humility and less shame.
They begin to rebuild trust in ways that feel safe, honest, and hopeful.

You don't need to rush this.
You don't need to perform this.
You don't even need to feel ready.

You only need to begin.

This is your invitation to slow down, breathe deeply, and step into a process many couples have walked before you — one that has helped people reconnect after both small ruptures and life-altering injuries.

Healing the heart isn't about forgetting what happened.
It's about understanding it, honoring it, and allowing it to lead you somewhere deeper, steadier, and more secure.

HOW TO USE THIS WORKBOOK

A Gentle Guide for Moving Through the HEART Model™ Together

This book is meant to be a companion — not a test, not a race, and not a rigid program you must complete perfectly. HEART is a model you return to again and again as life unfolds, as misunderstandings happen, and as your relationship grows.

Use this workbook in the way that feels most natural, spacious, and supportive for the two of you. The guidelines below are here to help, not to pressure.

1. Go at Your Own Pace

Some couples will move through one chapter a week.
Some will work one step into a single conversation.
Some will stay with one chapter for an entire season.

There is no right pace.
Move as slowly or as quickly as your hearts and nervous systems allow.

2. Don't Rush Healing or Forgiveness

Forgiveness is the hope, but **connection comes first**.

HEART creates the emotional conditions where forgiveness becomes possible, but you should never force it or pressure your partner to "get over it." Slow healing is still healing. Hesitation is information, not failure.

3. Start with Small Moments of Hurt

Before using HEART for big injuries, practice with smaller ones:

- a dismissive tone
- a forgotten detail
- a moment of disconnection
- a misunderstanding

Practicing on smaller hurts builds safety, trust, and confidence. Then, when deeper wounds arise, you already know the rhythm and language.

4. For Major Injuries, Don't Go It Alone

Some injuries in a relationship carry a different weight.
Examples include:

- infidelity or long-term affairs
- significant secret-keeping (hidden debt, double lives, undisclosed relationships)
- addictions that have impacted the relationship (substances, pornography, gambling, etc.)
- repeated betrayal of agreed-upon boundaries
- patterns of emotional, verbal, or spiritual harm

You *can* use the HEART Model™ to help you talk about and process these injuries — but it is **not** wise to walk through them alone as a couple without support.

For major ruptures, this workbook is best used:

- in the presence of a licensed therapist,
- in couples counseling or intensives,
- or with another trained professional who can help you pace the work, support regulation, and protect safety.

HEART is a powerful tool for forgiveness and repair, but it is not a substitute for trauma-informed care or safety planning. If there is ongoing abuse, coercion, or danger, your first step is securing safety and support — not jumping straight into repair work.

5. It's Okay to Pause Anytime

If emotions rise, if one of you feels flooded, or if you sense defensiveness or shutdown:

⮂ Pause.

⮂ Breathe.

⮂ Ground your body.

⮂ Come back when you both feel more regulated.

A regulated conversation is always more productive than a rushed one.

6. Use the Worksheets as Tools, Not Tests

The worksheets are here to support you, not to grade you.

You can:

⮂ do them together or separately

⮂ write your answers or simply talk them out

⮂ skip pages that don't fit right now

⮂ return to them again later

⮂ bring them into therapy or coaching sessions

Their purpose is simple: to help you deepen clarity and connection — nothing more, nothing less.

7. Expect to Circle Back

HEART is not strictly linear.

Some repairs will naturally require revisiting earlier steps, such as:

⮂ moving from **Release** back to **Empathy**

⮂ moving from **Acknowledgment** back to **Honor**

⮂ moving from **Turn Toward Repair** back to **Release**

This is normal and healthy.
It means you are working honestly, not rushing yourselves.

The Most Important Thing

You're not expected to master this.
You're invited to **practice** it.

HEART is a rhythm.
A posture.
A way of being with one another.

Use it as often as you need.
Return to it as many times as you must.

Let it be a gentle companion on your journey — especially in the moments when love feels stretched thin and you're looking for a way back to each other.

HEART AT A GLANCE

Your Quick-Reference Guide

The HEART Model™ is a simple, research-informed pathway for moving through hurt and back into connection. Each step helps you slow down, regulate, and rebuild emotional safety together.

Think of it as a rhythm you move through **as a team**, with different steps meant for different roles in the moment of hurt.

H — HONOR THE HURT

Who this step is for: the one who was hurt.

This step is about giving clear, compassionate language to your pain. You're naming what happened and how it landed inside you — emotionally and meaning-wise — without minimizing, exploding, or blaming.

You're not attacking your partner's character; you're sharing your experience.

⮑ **Focus on:**

- What happened
- What you felt (emotion + body)
- What the moment seemed to mean about you, them, or the relationship

⮑ **Guiding question:**

> *"What did I feel, and what did this moment mean to me?"*

E — EMPATHIZE WITH THE EXPERIENCE

Who this step is for: the one who did the hurting (or the partner responding to the hurt).

Here, your job is to step into your partner's world. You're not deciding whether you agree with every detail; you're practicing emotional imagination — trying to feel how it might have been for them.

Empathy softens defenses, calms the nervous system, and creates enough safety for responsibility to land.

⮞ **Focus on:**

- Listening instead of explaining
- Impact instead of intention
- Reflecting feelings, not correcting facts

⮞ **Guiding question:**

- "If I were them, with their story and sensitivity, how might this have felt?"

A — ACKNOWLEDGE RESPONSIBILITY

Who this step is for: the one who did the hurting (or the one whose behavior contributed to the hurt).

This is the behavioral accountability step. You're naming your part — what you did, didn't do, or how you showed up — and how that impacted your partner. No excuses, no self-attack, no disappearing into shame.

You're not declaring yourself "the bad one." You're standing in the truth of your impact.

⮞ **Focus on:**

- Naming your behavior plainly
- Naming your partner's experience with empathy
- Offering regret without defense

⮞ **Guiding question:**

- "What part of this hurt did my choices contribute to — and am I willing to own that clearly?"

R — RELEASE THE RESENTMENT

Who this step is for: the one who was hurt.

This step is about gently loosening what your heart has been holding to stay safe. You are **not** saying it didn't matter or that it was okay. You're simply noticing where it may feel safe enough to soften — even a little.

Release is always a softening, never a forced sprint.

⮑ **Focus on:**

- Noticing what you're still carrying
- Naming the fear underneath the resentment
- Allowing yourself to let go in layers, at your own pace

⮑ **Guiding question:**

- "What part of this am I ready — even 5% — to loosen my grip on?"

T — TURN TOWARD REPAIR

Who this step is for: both partners together.

This is where you choose connection again — not through grand gestures, but through small, consistent turns toward each other. Repair is where intention becomes action: new behaviors, new patterns, new emotional memories.

You're asking, **"What does 'moving forward differently' actually look like between us?"**

⮑ **Focus on:**

- Naming small, doable changes
- Following through in concrete ways
- Checking in and adjusting over time

⮑ **Guiding question:**

- "What small turn toward each other can we make right now?"

HOW THE HEART MODEL™ WAS BORN

Before the HEART Model™ had a name, it lived quietly inside the therapy room. It showed up in moments where couples stopped repeating their predictable pattern and finally slowed down enough to understand what was happening inside themselves and each other. It appeared in the way partners softened at just the right moment, took responsibility with an open chest instead of a defensive tone, or allowed themselves to feel the weight of a wound they had caused.

I didn't invent HEART.
I discovered it.

I began noticing that the couples who healed most consistently — whether from a sharp moment of misunderstanding or a long-standing injury — were unintentionally following the same internal sequence. Regardless of gender, background, attachment style, or story, the emotional movement looked strikingly similar.

It almost always began the same way:
one partner finally found the courage to name what hurt instead of minimizing it.

Then, the other partner opened their heart just enough to imagine what was happening inside the one who was hurting — not perfectly, but sincerely.

Next came a moment of ownership: the partner who caused the hurt began to acknowl-edge their impact clearly, without hiding behind explanations or collapsing into shame.

Only then did resentment start to loosen its grip in the one who had been carrying it.

And eventually, there was a way back to each other — not through a grand gesture, but through a small, meaningful act of repair.

Five movements, with plenty of pauses and detours.
Five steps — rarely clean or linear, but still quietly unfolding.
Five shifts of the heart.

The process was anything but polished, yet over and over again, I watched this same quiet choreography emerge between couples. At some point I thought, *This can't be a coinci-dence.*

I started writing these movements or moments down. I took notes after sessions, circling the moments I knew had changed the emotional temperature in the room. I listened to how couples talked about repair. I paid attention to my own marriage, noticing the subtle shifts that helped Amber and me find our way back to each other when things felt tender, tight, or overwhelming.

Eventually a pattern emerged — not a formula, but a rhythm.

Honor.
Empathize.
Acknowledge.
Release.
Turn.

HEART.

Simple.
Memorable.
Human.

It felt less like creating a model and more like naming what was already true in every heal-ing process I had ever witnessed.

The HEART Model™ was born not because I needed something catchy, but because I need-ed something that actually worked — something couples could remember in the heat of conflict, something therapists, coaches and pastors could teach, something partners could return to when they were afraid or hurting or exhausted from trying.

Why We Needed a New Way Forward

As mentioned in the introduction, there are excellent forgiveness models in psychology — Enright's, Worthington's REACH, McCullough's meaning-making work. I value them deeply, and they've shaped therapeutic thinking for decades.

But they share one limitation: they were created for individuals, not couples.

Individual forgiveness is different from romantic relational repair.

In a relationship – particularly in a romantic relationship, forgiveness is not just an internal emotional shift — it is a **dyadic process** that involves two nervous systems, two histories, two attachment styles, two tender spots, two ways of protecting, and two ways of reaching for closeness.

The individual models didn't fully answer the questions I saw couples struggle with every day:

- "How do we do this together?"
- "How do we forgive without pretending nothing happened?"
- "How do I own my part without collapsing in shame?"
- "What if resentment is still loud in my body?"
- "What does repair actually look like?"
- "How do we find our way back to safety after a rupture?"

Couples needed a model that spoke directly to the relational and attachment-based experience of forgiveness — not just the internal experience of an individual trying to let go.

HEART fills that gap.

The Emotional Architecture Behind HEART

As HEART took shape, so did my understanding of why it worked so reliably.

Each step aligns with core principles of attachment science, Emotionally Focused Therapy, and relational neuroscience.

There is a natural emotional intelligence built into the sequence:

- **Honoring the Hurt** reduces limbic reactivity and grounds the experience in clarity instead of accusation.
- **Empathy** shifts partners out of their negative interactive pattern by softening threat responses.

◌ **Acknowledgment** creates accountability without shame — a prerequisite for trust.

◌ **Releasing Resentment** calms the nervous system and prevents emotional gridlock.

◌ **Turning Toward Repair** builds new emotional memory — the foundation of secure attachment.

HEART doesn't force forgiveness; it *prepares the heart* for it.
It lowers defenses.
It increases safety.
It creates conditions where forgiveness becomes possible — sometimes for the first time in years.

How This Workbook Will Guide You

You don't have to master the steps all at once.
You don't have to be perfect.
You don't have to get it right the first, fifth, or fifteenth time.

What matters is movement — gentle, consistent, honest movement back toward each other.

Each chapter that follows will walk you through one step of the HEART Model™:

◌ a vignette that shows what the step looks like in real life

◌ the emotional and relational purpose behind the step

◌ interactive worksheets to guide you through each step

◌ and the relational shifts that emerge when couples engage the process

The Promise of HEART

I've watched couples who felt hopeless rediscover tenderness.
I've watched walls that seemed impenetrable soften in a single moment of empathy.
I've watched couples who hadn't touched an old wound for decades finally honor it —
and find relief in places they had stopped believing healing was possible.

Repair is almost always possible when both partners show up with honesty, humility, and heart.

And this is where your journey begins — not with perfection, but with willingness.
Not with certainty, but with openness.
Not with pressure, but with the simple courage to take the next small step.

The steps are waiting.
Your relationship is ready.
Let's walk this path together.

The next chapter begins where healing always begins: **H — Honor the Hurt.**

02

HONOR THE HURT

▌Naming Pain Is the First Act of Healing

There is a moment in every relationship when hurt enters the room.

Sometimes it arrives quietly — a forgotten promise, a dismissive tone, a moment of inattention. Other times it arrives like a wave — a cutting remark, an emotional withdrawal, or a choice that violates trust.

However it comes, one truth remains: hurt that goes unacknowledged becomes hurt that grows.

Hurt that goes unacknowledged becomes hurt that grows.

Honoring the hurt is the beginning of every repair because you cannot heal what you refuse to name. Most of us were taught to move past pain quickly, to "not make a big deal," or to swallow our reactions so the relationship stays calm.

You cannot heal what you refuse to name.

But emotional injuries don't disappear when they're ignored; they internalize.

They become stories.

⮕ "He doesn't really care."

⮕ "I don't matter to her."

⮕ "I'm too much."

⮕ "I'm alone in this."

Honoring the hurt interrupts that story. It says, "This mattered. This impacted me. And my experience deserves to be seen."

Why This Step Matters

Honoring the hurt is not about assigning blame.
It's about clarity.

Before we go further, it's important to clarify: this step is primarily for the partner who was hurt. Honoring the hurt is about coming home to *your* truth, *your* body, and *your* experience. If you're the one who did the hurting, your main work in this phase is to make space, stay present, and listen. Your turn in this process comes in the later steps of HEART.

Honoring the hurt does two important things:

1. **It brings you back into contact with your own truth.**
   Instead of spiraling in irritation, withdrawal, or overreaction, you slow down long enough to understand what actually hurt and why. You stop arguing with yourself about whether you're "too sensitive" and start listening to what your body and heart are trying to tell you.

2. **It helps your partner see the impact without shame or attack.**
   When hurt is expressed clearly (not reactively), your partner can stay present instead of getting defensive or shutting down. You are naming impact, not prosecuting intent.

From a nervous system and attachment perspective, this step matters because your body doesn't accept shortcuts. Even if your mind says, "It's fine, let it go," your chest may still tighten, your stomach still drops, your sleep still gets restless.

Underneath, your attachment system is asking questions like:

⮕ "Am I safe with you?"

⮕ "Do I matter?"

⮕ "Will you show up for me when I'm vulnerable?"

Honoring the hurt brings those questions into the light, where they can be met instead of managed alone in the dark.

Sofia and David

A moment of hurt

Sofia and David had been doing better lately. After a rough season marked by miscommunication and financial stress, they were finally finding small moments of connection. One night, as they were getting ready for bed, Sofia shared something vulnerable about feeling insecure at work.

David, exhausted, scrolling mindlessly, muttered without looking up, "You'll be fine. Don't stress."

That was it.
A small moment.
Barely a sentence.

But Sofia felt something collapse inside her.

Her body stiffened.
Her throat tightened.
Her chest burned with a familiar ache — the ache of feeling invisible.

She didn't yell.
She didn't protest.
She didn't say anything at all.

She simply turned off her bedside lamp and shut down.

The next morning, when they sat in my office, David said, "I don't understand. I didn't say anything mean. I just told you you'd be fine."

Sofia looked at him, tears forming.

"It wasn't what you said," she whispered. "It was that I really needed you to see me. And you didn't."

That is the moment we begin HEART.

Sofia wasn't attacking.
She wasn't blaming.
She was naming the impact.
She was honoring the hurt.

This step is simply a truth-telling step.

Not emotional dumping.
Not lecturing.
Not proving.
Not rehashing every detail.

Just naming the wound.

It sounds like:

- ➲ "When that happened, something inside me tightened."
- ➲ "This brought up an old hurt for me."
- ➲ "I felt dismissed when you said that."
- ➲ "I felt alone in that moment."
- ➲ "I felt scared you didn't care."
- ➲ "The part that hurt the most was…"

Honoring the hurt is about describing the emotional and relational impact, not accusing your partner of intent. *Impact without accusation is the doorway to connection.*

Impact without accusation is the doorway to connection.

| **What Honoring the Hurt Is Not**

Because this step is so vulnerable, it's easy to confuse honoring hurt with a few things it's not:

- ➲ **It's not a character assassination.**
  "You're a terrible partner" is not the same as, "I felt abandoned when you walked away."
- ➲ **It's not a courtroom transcript.**
  You don't have to get every detail "exactly right" for your experience to be valid. You're sharing how it landed inside you.
- ➲ **It's not erasing your partner's perspective.**
  Their story matters too. We're just not doing both at once.

⇨ **It's not staying in harm's way.**
   If there is ongoing abuse, honoring the hurt may mean acknowledging it clearly
   enough to seek outside help, set boundaries, or leave.

You can honor your hurt and still hold onto your partner's humanity.

Why We Avoid Honoring the Hurt

Many people struggle with this step because:

⇨ They fear being "too sensitive."

⇨ They don't want to start conflict.

⇨ They were taught to keep the peace.

⇨ They fear their partner won't receive it well.

⇨ They don't want to be blamed for being hurt.

⇨ They're afraid the hurt reveals too much vulnerability.

⇨ They worry, "If I really feel this, I'll drown in it," or, "If I admit this mattered, I'll have
   to make a hard decision."

So we do what humans do best: we protect.

We minimize.
We rationalize.
We tell ourselves it wasn't a big deal.

We scroll, pour another drink, overwork, make jokes, or move on.

But avoiding the hurt doesn't keep the peace — it delays the repair.

Avoiding the hurt doesn't keep the peace — it delays the repair.

Underneath the avoidance, the nervous system is still busy, storing this moment next to
other moments that felt similar. Over time, the story grows: "I'm alone in this," "I don't
matter," "If I speak up, it'll only make things worse."

Honoring the hurt is what starts to loosen that story.

The Deeper Work: Connecting the Moment to the Meaning

When you honor the hurt, you're naming not only what happened externally, but what it activated internally.

For Sofia, it wasn't the sentence. It was the story underneath it: "I don't matter enough to pause. I'm on my own."

Honoring the hurt requires slowing down enough to ask:
"What did this moment mean to me?"

That meaning is almost always tied to:

- earlier experiences
- unmet attachment needs
- old relational wounds
- moments where we felt unseen or unheard

This is why honoring the hurt is not superficial work.
It is brave work.

A Closer Look Inside the Moment

Let's go deeper into Sofia's experience.

When David brushed her off, her body reacted before her brain formed a sentence. This is how emotional memory works. Our nervous system stores past relational injuries and pulls them forward in an instant.

The hurt wasn't about that single moment.
It was about history.
It was about longing.
It was about needing presence during vulnerability.

When couples don't honor hurt, they end up arguing about surface-level details:

- "You're overreacting."
- "I didn't mean it like that."
- "You're making a big deal out of nothing."

But the hurt was never about the surface.
It was about the heart.

How to Honor the Hurt in a Healthy Way

Let's look at three elements that need to be present to honor the hurt in a healthy way:

1. **Slowing down**
    Not reacting instantly.
    Pausing long enough to identify what actually hurt.

2. **Naming the feeling**
    Using emotional language, not behavioral accusations.
    "I felt small and alone," not, "You're so selfish."

3. **Naming the meaning**
    Sharing the internal story without making your partner the villain.
    "It made me believe I don't matter," rather than, "You obviously don't care."

For the One Who Was Hurt

If you're the one carrying the injury, honoring the hurt might feel risky.

It's easier, in some ways, to stay guarded: "If I don't name it, I can't be rejected in it."

But honoring your hurt doesn't make you needy or dramatic. It makes you honest. It gives your partner (and you) a chance to meet what's real instead of dancing around what's unspoken.

You deserve to have your pain seen. You deserve to know if your partner is capable of showing up there with you.

For the One Who Caused the Hurt

If you're the one who caused the hurt, this step can stir up shame.

You might think:

- "I already apologized. Why are we still here?"
- "It wasn't my intention to hurt anyone. Can't they see that?"
- "If I really take this in, I'll hate myself."
- "If I let them talk about this, we'll never move on."

Honoring the hurt is not your punishment. In this step, it's not even about *you* yet — it's about making room for your partner's *experience* to be heard clearly.

Your job here is simple and hard at the same time: stay, listen, and let the impact land.

You don't have to explain, correct the details, or share your side right now. That work comes later, when we move into **Empathize with the Experience** and **Acknowledge Responsibility.**

For now, you're not the one holding the mic. You're the one *bearing witness.*

You are not the worst thing you've done here. You are the person choosing to sit still, listen, and allow your partner's reality to matter. That choice matters more than you know.

You've just walked through the *why* and the *how* of honoring the hurt. Now it's time to gently name your own.

The next page is **Worksheet 1: Honor the Hurt**, and it's designed **for the partner who was hurt** in this particular situation. Take your time with it. Let it help you put words to what happened, how it landed in your body, and what it began to mean inside your story.

Impact Statement Reflection Sheet

Honoring the hurt means naming the emotional impact without minimizing, rushing, or blaming.

Part 1: What Happened

Describe the the moment of impact.

What part of this moment stands out the most?

Part 2: What You Felt

List your emotions: (Sad, angry, guilt, shame, fear, disgust, contempt)

1.   4.

2.   5.

3.   6.

Which emotion was strongest?

Where did you feel this in your body? (Chest, stomach, shoulders, throat)

Part 3: What It Touched in Your Story

Did this moment remind you of anything from your past?

Part 4: What You Needed

What did you need emotionally in that moment?

Part 5: Impact Statement

"When ____________ happened, I felt _____________ because it made me believe __________."

Part 6: Gentle Check-In

What do you feel now?

What do you need next?

Next Step

You've now honored what this moment meant to you. The next worksheet in HEART is for your partner to complete as they practice the second step: **Empathize with the Experience.**

What This Step Makes Possible

When you honor the hurt, you create emotional clarity.

Clarity reduces conflict.
Clarity increases connection.
Clarity prepares the heart for empathy.

This is why H must come before E.

You can't empathize with something that hasn't been named.
You can't understand a wound that is still hidden.
You can't repair what hasn't been identified.

Honoring the hurt opens the door to every step that follows.

Most couples skip this step — not because they don't want healing, but because naming hurt feels vulnerable.

It feels exposing.
It feels like admitting you were impacted.

But this step is the hinge on which everything else turns.

This is the moment where the emotional fog begins to lift.

Some hurts are small.
Some are layered.
Some have nothing to do with the present moment and everything to do with the stories that shaped you long before your relationship began.

Naming the hurt isn't about placing blame.
It's about locating the wound so healing becomes possible.

And here's the quiet truth most couples don't realize: **The moment you can say, "This is where it hurt," the relationship is already beginning to heal.**

You've stepped out of confusion.
You've stepped toward presence.
You've stepped into honesty.

You've opened the door to empathy — the next step in this journey.

Empathy cannot be forced.
It cannot be demanded.

It can only emerge when the emotional landscape is clear enough for compassion to land.

By honoring the hurt, you make empathy possible. You set the stage for your partner to understand you — not defensively, not reactively, but human to human, heart to heart.

This is where healing begins to take shape.

And now, with clarity on the table, we can move toward the second step: **Empathize with the Experience.**

03

EMPATHIZE WITH THE EXPERIENCE

Seeing Through Your Partner's Eyes Without Losing Yourself

Once the hurt has been honored, the next step is the one that changes everything: **empathy**.

Empathy is often misunderstood. People assume it means taking the blame, agreeing with every detail, or collapsing your own needs to make room for your partner's pain. That's not empathy — that's self-erasure.

Empathy is not surrender.
Empathy is not saying, "You're right, I'm wrong."
Empathy is not absorbing all responsibility.

Empathy is **presence**.
Empathy is **curiosity**.
Empathy is the movement of the heart toward understanding.

When you empathize with your partner, you aren't agreeing with their interpretation — you're acknowledging their **experience.** And experience is always valid, even when the facts feel complicated.

When you empathize with your partner, you aren't agreeing with their *interpretation* — you're acknowledging their *experience*.

Empathy says:

- ➲ "I see how this moment impacted you."
- ➲ "I can feel the tenderness beneath your reaction."
- ➲ "I understand why that hurt."
- ➲ "You make sense to me."

Empathy is the antidote to defensiveness.
Empathy is the bridge.
Empathy is the moment walls turn into windows.

Empathy is the antidote to defensiveness.

▌Why This Step Matters

When a partner shares hurt, the other partner often reacts instinctively with:

- ➲ "I didn't mean it like that."
- ➲ "You're misreading me."
- ➲ "You always think the worst."
- ➲ "You're blowing this out of proportion."

These reactions are not usually malicious; they are **protective**.

Humans defend where we feel shame.

But defensiveness stops connection instantly. The hurt partner's nervous system reads those responses as, "My pain is too much," or, "I'm not safe to be honest here."

Empathy softens shame, reduces defensiveness, and communicates: "You don't have to protect yourself from me. We're on the same team."

On a brain level, empathy helps calm the **amygdala** — the fear center. On a body level, it supports **co-regulation**: two nervous systems moving from threat back toward safety together. Empathy prepares both partners for the next steps of responsibility and repair.

Sofia and David

Stepping into each other's experience.

After Sofia shared her hurt honestly, David sat quiet for a moment. His first instinct was to explain — to tell her he was tired, stressed, distracted. To defend his intentions.

Instead, he took a breath.
He remembered what we had talked about.
He turned toward her.

"I didn't see that I brushed you off," he said slowly.
"But hearing you say that… it makes sense why that felt painful.
You were trying to open up, and I wasn't there.
I can see how that would feel lonely."

Sofia's shoulders dropped.
Her eyes softened.

Not because David got it perfect.
Not because he took the blame.

But because he **saw her.**

That is the power of empathy.

It shifts the emotional climate instantly.

Emotional Imagination

Empathy is *emotional imagination*. It's picturing what the moment felt like from your partner's side of the world.

> *Empathy is emotional imagination.*

Here are empathy-aligned statements that build connection:

- "I can understand why that hurt."
- "I didn't realize that moment felt so heavy for you."
- "Thank you for telling me — it helps me understand you more."
- "I can see how this connects to something deeper."
- "If I were in your shoes, I might feel the same."

➲ "You make sense to me."

Empathy requires two key shifts:

1. From explaining to listening
2. From correcting the story to understanding the emotion

You don't have to agree with the details to empathize.

What Gets in the Way of Empathy?

Several internal blocks make empathy difficult:

1. **Defensiveness**
   We want to protect our character and intentions.

2. **Shame**
   It's hard to face the idea that we hurt someone we love.

3. **Fear of being blamed**
   Many partners equate empathy with taking all responsibility.

4. **Emotional flooding**
   When our nervous system ramps up, empathy becomes almost impossible. We're in survival mode, not connection mode.

5. **Old wounds being activated**
   Sometimes your partner's hurt touches your own unhealed story — rejection, criticism, not being enough — and your system reacts to *that* as much as to the moment in front of you.

The Deeper Work: Empathy as Attachment Repair

Empathy is not just a social skill — it is an **attachment repair move**.

In attachment science, every couple lives inside a bond shaped by two core questions:

➲ "Are you there for me?"
➲ "Am I safe with you?"

When those questions are answered with presence, responsiveness, and warmth, the nervous system settles and connection strengthens. When they're not, the bond becomes strained, and partners fall into protective patterns: demanding, withdrawing, shutting down, or managing alone.

Empathy is the antidote to that strain.
It is the moment the bond begins to heal.

When partners offer genuine empathy, it:

⮑ reduces perceived threat

⮑ signals emotional availability

⮑ increases felt safety

⮑ enhances bonding

⮑ decreases anxiety

⮑ decreases shutdown

⮑ creates the conditions for risk-taking and vulnerability

When couples practice empathy consistently, the entire relational pattern shifts.

The partner who once felt unheard begins to soften.
The partner who once pulled away feels safe enough to stay present.

Connection becomes a shared rhythm instead of a tug-of-war.

Going Back to Sofia and David

When David empathized, Sofia didn't feel dramatic, needy, or irrational anymore.

She felt human.
She felt understood.
She felt safe enough to keep going.

And David?

He felt relief.

Once empathy was present, he realized he didn't need to defend himself. His intention could be understood later.

But first, she needed his **presence**.

Empathy took them from disconnection to possibility.

Empathy takes you from disconnection to possibility.

How to Empathize with Your Partner's Experience

Three simple actions make empathy possible:

1. **Slow the moment down**
   You cannot empathize while rushing or reacting. Take a breath. Pause before you speak. Let your partner's words land.

2. **Reflect what you hear**
   Not word-for-word — emotionally.
   "You felt alone. I get that."
   "You felt foolish and exposed. That makes sense."

3. **Imagine the moment from their internal vantage point**
   Ask yourself: *If I were them, with their history, their sensitivities, their nervous system… would this hurt?*

   The answer is almost always yes.

Empathy is not about deciding whether you *would* have reacted the same way. It's about recognizing that *given who they are and what they've lived*, their reaction is understandable.

For the One Who Was Hurt

If you're the partner who has been carrying the hurt, receiving empathy can feel both relieving and scary.

Part of you may think:

➲ "If I let this in, I might cry and never stop."

➲ "What if they only say this once and then go back to the old pattern?"

➲ "Do I trust this?"

You don't have to swallow empathy all at once. You can take it in slowly, like sips of water when you've been thirsty for a long time.

For the One Who Hurt

If you're the partner who caused the injury, offering empathy can stir up your own pain.

You might think:

➲ "If I really see their hurt, I'll drown in guilt."

⮑ "If I validate this, it means I'm the bad one."

⮑ "If I empathize, they'll never let this go."

Empathy is not a guilty plea. It's a **human** response.

You can say, "You make sense," without saying, "I'm irredeemable."
You can say, "I see how that hurt," without saying, "I am only what I did."

In fact, the ability to offer empathy is one of the clearest signs that you are **more** than your worst moment. It shows that you are capable of growth, responsibility, and care.

You've just explored what empathy asks of *both* of you — the courage to let your hurt be seen, and the courage to stay present with the impact you've had.

The next page, **Worksheet 2: Empathize with the Experience**, is primarily for **the partner who did the hurting** in this situation. Use it to slow down, imagine the moment from your partner's side, and put words to how you understand their experience.

Let's begin.

EMPATHIZE WITH THE EXPERIENCE

Partner Empathy Mapping Sheet

Empathy is seeing the moment through your partner's eyes — not agreeing, but understanding.

Part 1: What Happened for Them

How would they describe what happened?

Part 2: What They Felt

Which emotions might they have felt?

Part 3: What They Feared

What fear or tenderness might have been touched?

Part 4: What They Needed

What emotional need was underneath their reaction?

Part 5: How Their Behavior Makes Sense

What might explain their reaction (not justify — explain)?

Part 6: What You See Differently Now

What do you now understand that you didn't before?

Part 7: Empathy Statement

"I can imagine that when ___________ happened, you felt __________ because ___________."

Part 8: Gentle Check-In

What feels different in you?

How do you want to show up now?

Next Step

If you were the partner practicing empathy on this worksheet, your next step is to complete the following worksheet: **Acknowledge Responsibility.**

What Empathy Makes Possible

Empathy is what makes acknowledgment (the next step) meaningful instead of mechanical.

Without empathy:

- acknowledgment lacks heart
- responsibility feels forced
- repair feels hollow
- resentment remains

With empathy:

- truth lands gently
- responsibility becomes relational
- repair becomes mutual
- resentment softens naturally

Once empathy is present, something shifts in the nervous system — in both partners.

The one who was hurt feels understood enough to soften.
The one who offered empathy feels safe enough to stay open.

The emotional fog clears just enough for truth to land without instant defensiveness or crushing shame.

Empathy creates the safety.
Responsibility creates the movement.

Together, they turn two nervous systems toward healing instead of self-protection.

This is why the HEART Model moves in this order.

Empathy softens the emotional ground so acknowledgment can take root — not as a performance, but as a genuine act of connection.

You don't have to be perfect to take responsibility.
You only have to be present.

Now that your partner feels seen, and now that your heart is open enough to understand their experience, you're ready to step into the next stage of repair — **Acknowledge Responsibility**.

Let's go there together.

04

ACKNOWLEDGE RESPONSIBILITY

Taking Ownership Without Shame, Self-Protection, or Collapse

If empathy softens the emotional ground, acknowledgment is where seeds of healing take root. This is the step most couples fear, resist, or misunderstand — often because they equate responsibility with guilt, shame, or being "the bad one."

In some ways, this step can feel similar to *Honor the Hurt* — we're still talking about what happened and how it landed. But there's an important difference:

- **Honor the Hurt** is about naming the experience the injured partner encountered.
- **Acknowledge Responsibility** is about naming the other partner's part in causing or contributing to that wound.

Honor gives language to pain.
Acknowledgment gives language to **behavioral accountability**.

Acknowledgment is not confession.
It is not punishment.
It is not surrender.

Acknowledgment is courage.
Acknowledgment is integrity.
Acknowledgment is emotional adulthood.

When you acknowledge responsibility, you are not declaring yourself wrong or defective. You are simply recognizing the real impact of your actions, inactions, tone, absence, or timing — even when your intentions were good.

This is the step where partners stop debating the facts and start recognizing the effect.

In relationships, effect matters more than intent.

Why This Step Matters

A nervous system that feels unseen will protest.
A nervous system that feels blamed will defend.
A nervous system that feels acknowledged will soften.

Acknowledgment defuses defensiveness by telling your partner:

- ➲ "You're not crazy."
- ➲ "You're not making this up."
- ➲ "Your hurt makes sense."
- ➲ "I'm not running from this."

And perhaps most importantly: *"I care about how this impacted you."*

This single step rebuilds trust faster than any grand gesture ever could, because it tells your partner, *"I'm willing to stand in the truth with you, not hide from it."*

Returning to Sofia and David

A moment of responsibility opening the door to repair.

After empathizing with Sofia's experience, David took a breath. His shoulders dropped into a posture of willingness. You could feel the shift — from self-protection to presence.

"I see now that I wasn't really with you," he said.
"When you shared something vulnerable, I stayed distracted. I didn't look up. I didn't pause. I didn't make space for you. And I'm sorry for the impact that had."

Notice what he didn't say:

- He didn't say, "I didn't mean to."
- He didn't say, "You took it the wrong way."
- He didn't say, "You know I'm tired."
- He didn't say, "This is just how I am."
- He didn't say, "You're overreacting."

He stayed with **impact**, not intention.
He stayed with **behavior**, not defense.

Sofia immediately exhaled.
It's the exhale that happens when the heart says, *"Okay. I'm not alone in this anymore."*

The Mistake Most Couples Make

Often, partners try to defend their character instead of acknowledging the moment. It sounds like:

- "I didn't mean it."
- "I would never hurt you on purpose."
- "You're reading me wrong."
- "You know I love you."

All of these statements may be true.
But none of them help.

Why? Because they center your **intention** rather than your partner's **experience**.

Acknowledgment is not about proving your goodness by defending intention. It's about addressing the experience of your partners pain.

What Acknowledgment Actually Sounds Like

Healthy acknowledgment contains three elements:

1. **Naming the behavior or moment honestly**

   "I interrupted you while you were sharing something important."

2. **Naming the impact with empathy**

   "My behavior made you feel dismissed."

3. **Expressing regret without self-defense**

   "And I'm sorry for the way that affected you."

This is clean, grounded responsibility.
No collapse.
No shame spiral.
No self-attack.

Just truth with compassion — and ownership without excuses.

If *Honor the Hurt* is about giving accurate words to the **pain**, *Acknowledge Responsibility* is about giving accurate words to **your part in that pain**.

▌ The Internal Work of Taking Responsibility

Acknowledgment requires emotional regulation. To stay with responsibility, you must quiet the urge to:

- ⮱ explain
- ⮱ justify
- ⮱ minimize
- ⮱ defend
- ⮱ debate
- ⮱ shift the focus
- ⮱ retaliate
- ⮱ collapse into self-loathing

This is why responsibility is not always intuitive — but it can be learned.

To acknowledge responsibility well, you have to make peace with imperfection. You have to accept the truth that good partners sometimes cause hurt — not because they are bad people, but because they are human.

> *Good partners sometimes cause hurt — not because they are bad people, but because they are human.*

When you can hold that truth, responsibility becomes far less scary and far more freeing. You're no longer proving you're flawless; you're proving you're trustworthy enough to tell the truth.

How to Stay Steady While Owning Your Part

Here are a few regulation moves that help you stay present while taking responsibility:

- ➲ **Breathe slower than you normally would.**
  Inhale gently, exhale a little longer. This signals to your nervous system, *"We're safe enough to stay."*
- ➲ **Plant your feet.**
  Feel the ground under you. Let your body know you don't have to run or fight right now.
- ➲ **Use compassionate self-talk.**

  - "I'm allowed to make mistakes."
  - "I can own this without hating myself."
  - "This is part of being a real partner."

These small internal shifts make it possible to say, "I see my part," without disappearing into shame.

Why Responsibility Isn't the Same as Taking All the Blame

Some partners avoid acknowledgment because they fear being swallowed by it. They believe:

- ➲ "If I admit this hurt you, it means the whole thing is my fault."
- ➲ "If I admit my part, your part won't matter anymore."
- ➲ "If I say I'm sorry, it means I'm the problem."

None of that is true.

Acknowledgment is not binary.
It is not a courtroom.
It is not an admission of total guilt.

It is simply the moment you say: **"I see the part I played, and I'm willing to own it."**

In healthy relationships, responsibility is shared.
But responsibility must be taken **one partner at a time**.

You don't have to carry the whole story to carry your part with honesty.

The Neuroscience of Acknowledgment

When responsibility is taken sincerely:

⮑ the hurt partner's amygdala — the fear center of the brain — calms down

⮑ the defensive partner's shame decreases

⮑ mirror neurons activate empathy loops

⮑ oxytocin (the bonding hormone) increases

⮑ threat responses soften

⮑ vulnerability becomes safe again

Responsibility literally changes the emotional chemistry of a conversation. The body hears:

"We're not in a fight for survival anymore.
We're in a process of repair."

The Shift in Sofia

When David acknowledged the moment clearly — no excuses, no self-preservation — something happened inside Sofia that happens inside every partner who has longed to be understood:

⮑ Her nervous system reset.

⮑ Her stomach unclenched.

⮑ Her breath deepened.

⮑ Her shoulders softened.

Instead of guarding herself, she leaned slightly toward him.

This is the posture of reconnection — the body saying,
"Okay. We can heal this."

For the One Who Was Hurt

If you're the one who's been carrying the hurt, acknowledgment can feel like water in the desert.

You may have spent months or years:

⮑ trying to explain the impact,

⮑ doubting your own reality,

⮑ feeling like you're "too sensitive" or "too much,"

⊃ wondering if your pain will ever truly matter.

When your partner says, "I see that when I did _______, it made you feel _______, and I'm sorry for that impact," you might feel a mix of relief and grief.

Relief, because you're finally not alone in the story.
Grief, because now that it's named, the weight of what you carried becomes clearer.

Both are normal.

You don't have to rush to forgiveness or say, "It's okay." You're allowed to take in acknowledgment slowly, to let your body register:

"I'm not crazy. It did happen. And they see it."

Sometimes, that alone is a massive part of healing.

For the One Who Hurt

If you're the partner taking responsibility, this step can stir up deep fear:

⊃ "If I really own this, I'll drown in shame."
⊃ "If I say I see it, they'll never let it go."
⊃ "If I admit this, it proves I'm the villain."

Here's the truth: avoiding responsibility keeps you stuck in shame.
Owning your part is what actually moves you out of it.

Avoiding responsibility keeps you stuck in shame.

You are not your worst moment.
You are the person who is choosing to face it.

When you say, "I see the impact I had," you're not agreeing that you are broken or unworthy. You're agreeing that your partner's pain is real and that you want to live in line with your values from here forward.

That's integrity.
That's growth.
That's love in action.

This is the step where you practice being trustworthy — not by being perfect, but by being accountable.

You've now seen what acknowledgment does inside *both* of you — how it can feel like relief for the one who was hurt, and like vulnerable courage for the one who caused the injury.

The next page, **Worksheet 3: Acknowledge Responsibility**, is designed **for the partner who did the hurting** in this situation. Use it to name your part clearly, focus on impact rather than intent, and practice taking ownership without collapsing into shame.

ACKNOWLEDGE RESPONSIBILITY

Ownership & Repair Planning Sheet

Responsibility is not blame — it is clarity, humility, and a willingness to see your part.

Part 1: What You Contributed

What did you say or do that played a role in the hurt?

Part 2: Your Intention

What were you *trying* to do in that moment?

Part 3: The Impact

How did your partner experience your behavior?

Part 4: Your Ownership Statement

Complete the sentence:

"I see how my _________ affected you by _________, and I take responsibility for _________."

Part 5: What You Would Do Differently

If you could redo the moment, how would you show up?

Part 6: The Repair You Can Offer

What small, meaningful action can you take to repair the damage?

Next Step

The next worksheet, **Release the Resentment,** is for the partner who was hurt.

What This Step Makes Possible

Acknowledgment changes the emotional weather of the relationship.

When you take responsibility with clarity and compassion, something important happens inside both of you. The partner who was hurt no longer has to fight to prove the injury is real. The partner who caused the hurt no longer has to hide behind defensiveness or shame. The nervous system moves from protection to possibility.

But acknowledgment, on its own, is not the end of the journey.

Even when your hurt is finally seen and validated, the residue of pain often lingers. Resentment — whether loud and obvious or quiet and buried — doesn't vanish just because someone said, "I'm sorry," or, "I see the impact now."

That's because resentment is, at its core, a protector.
It steps in to keep you from being hurt again.
It holds onto the story so you don't forget what happened.
It keeps distance where closeness once felt dangerous.

Responsibility opens the door.
Release is what allows you to walk through it.

The next step in The HEART Model™ is not about forcing forgiveness or pretending the hurt never mattered. It's about gently loosening resentment's grip so your heart is no longer organized around the injury.

You're not erasing the past.
You're making space for a different future.

With acknowledgment in place, your body has what it needs to even consider letting go: safety, validation, and truth. Now we can turn toward one of the hardest, most liberating parts of this process:

Release the Resentment.

05

RELEASE THE RESENTMENT

▌Letting Go of What No Longer Protects the Relationship

Releasing resentment is often the hardest step of the HEART Model™ — not because people are stubborn, unforgiving, or unwilling to move on, but because resentment has done an important job for a long time.

Resentment is a **protector**.

It shields you from vulnerability.
It prevents you from getting hurt again.
It keeps you alert, guarded, ready.
It gives structure to pain that felt chaotic.

Resentment is often what the heart holds when it doesn't yet feel safe.

Resentment is often what the heart holds when it doesn't yet feel safe.

This is why telling someone to "just let it go" never works.

Resentment can't be forced out.
It must be **released** — gently, gradually, honestly — and only when the heart feels safe enough to loosen its grip.

Releasing the hurt is not the same as forgetting.
It is not pretending the hurt didn't matter.
It is not saying what happened was okay.
It is not rushing to forgiveness because you're uncomfortable with tension.

Releasing resentment means: "I am choosing not to keep rehearsing this wound as a way to protect myself."

You still remember the story. You still honor what it cost you. You simply stop letting the hurt run the whole show.

Why This Step Matters

Resentment is like emotional residue — it sticks to our interpretations, our tone, our reactions, our expectations. You can be doing everything "right" in your relationship and still feel the heaviness of old pain coloring the present moment.

If resentment stays, even empathy and acknowledgment begin to lose their effectiveness.

> Resentment is like emotional residue — it sticks to our interpretations, our tone, our reactions, our expectations.

It shows up as:

➲ irritation over small things

➲ quickness to assume the worst

➲ emotional distance

➲ a slow erosion of tenderness

➲ difficulty trusting change

➲ keeping score

➲ reliving the moment again and again

Resentment reshapes the emotional landscape of the relationship.
Releasing it reopens the possibility of closeness.

From a nervous system perspective, resentment is like staying half-braced for impact — muscles tight, guard up, scanning for danger. Release doesn't mean pretending danger never existed; it means your body finally believes, *"For now, I'm safe enough to soften."*

Back to Sofia and David

A heart finally ready to loosen the grip.

After David acknowledged the impact of his dismissal with sincerity — clear, grounded, shame-free — Sofia felt something inside her body shift.

She didn't feel pressure to forgive.
She didn't feel rushed to "move on."

She simply felt… safer.

For the first time since that moment in their bedroom, she believed he saw her.

She said quietly, "Part of me wants to hold onto this, because it hurt. But another part of me feels like I can let go a little. I don't want to carry this between us."

That sentence — "I don't want to carry this between us" — is the beginning of release.

It's not a grand statement.
It's not a final resolution.
It's not perfection.

It's an **opening**.

The release of resentment is always a softening, never a snap.

The release of resentment is always a softening, never a snap.

What Resentment Really Protects

Resentment has its roots in **fear:**

- fear that the hurt will happen again
- fear that your partner won't change
- fear that your pain doesn't matter
- fear that you will have to carry the weight alone
- fear that acknowledging repair will make you vulnerable again

When resentment loosens, fear loosens with it.

But resentment won't release unless the heart feels held, seen, and safe.
This is why the steps before it matter so much.

Honoring the hurt says, "My pain is real."
Empathy says, "You make sense to me."
Acknowledgment says, "I see and own my impact."

Release says, "Given all of that, I don't want this hurt to run my heart anymore."

What Releasing Resentment Actually Looks Like

Releasing resentment is not a single moment — it is a series of small internal shifts:

- You stop replaying the worst version of the story.
- You stop using the hurt as evidence against your partner's growth.
- You stop letting this moment define your partner's entire character.
- You stop carrying the emotional memory into unrelated conflicts.
- You stop gripping the pain as your only form of protection.

It may begin with a sentence as simple as:

- "I think I'm ready to soften."
- "I don't want this to separate us anymore."
- "I'm willing to try releasing some of this."
- "I don't feel stuck in it the same way."
- "I think I can let go of part of this today."

Release is not all-or-nothing.
Release is layered.

The Internal Work of Letting Go

To release resentment, you must engage two practices:

1. **Internal honesty**
   "What pain am I still holding onto, and why?"

2. **Internal permission**
   "Is it safe enough now to loosen this grip?"

Resentment does not release through pressure — it releases through permission.

Resentment does not release through pressure — it releases through permission.

This isn't about forcing yourself to feel ready; it's about checking in with the part of you that has been guarding the wound and asking, "What do you need now?"

The Body Knows When It's Safe to Let Go

Resentment is not just cognitive — it is stored physically.

Tight jaw.
Shallow breath.
Clenched fists.
A knot in the stomach.
A heaviness in the chest.

As acknowledgment lands, the nervous system shifts:

- breathing deepens
- shoulders soften
- the jaw releases
- emotional temperature lowers
- presence increases

This physiological shift is what makes emotional release possible.

Your body knows when it's safe to let go.
Your heart follows.

Continuing Sofia & David's Story

As David's acknowledgment sank in, Sofia's mind stopped rehearsing the old loop: *"He doesn't care. He's not there for me. I'm alone in this."*

Her body registered the change before her mind did:

Her shoulders dropped.
Her heart rate slowed.
Her eyes softened.
Her breath deepened.

And then she said something profound for her relationship: *"I don't want to hold onto the story that you don't care. I know you do."*

This is release.
A quiet return to truth.
A loosening of the fear.
A restoration of trust-in-progress.

How to Support the Process of Release

Here are three ways partners can support healthy release:

1. **Reassure safety without pushing for closure**
   "I'm here. Take all the time you need."
   "You don't have to rush this for me."

2. **Validate the complexity of letting go**
   "It makes sense that this was hard to release. It mattered."
   "I know this hurt is layered — I don't expect it to vanish overnight."

3. **Continue making small repair moves**
   Following through.
   Showing up consistently.
   Staying emotionally available.

Consistency builds safety.
Safety makes release sustainable.

For the One Who Was Hurt

If you're the one who was hurt, resentment may have felt like your only shield.

It might have sounded like:

➲ "If I stay mad, I can't be blindsided again."

➲ "If I keep this close, I won't forget what happened."

➲ "If I soften, they might hurt me in the same way."

Your resentment has been trying to protect you.

So when you consider releasing it, you might feel exposed, shaky, or even disloyal to your past self — the version of you who went through the pain.

Here's what I want you to hear: You can honor what you went through **and** allow your body to rest.

Letting go of resentment does not mean:

⮑ that what happened was okay,

⮑ that you'd tolerate it again,

⮑ or that your boundaries no longer matter.

It means:

⮑ "I believe I am safer now."

⮑ "I trust myself to speak up sooner."

⮑ "I'm ready for my heart to be organized around more than this wound."

You're allowed to go slowly.
You're allowed to release 5% at a time.
You're allowed to say, "I'm softening, but I still need you to stay consistent."

Your pace is part of your wisdom.

For the One Who Hurt

If you're the partner who caused the injury, this step can be both hopeful and terrifying.

You might think:

⮑ "If they really let this go, do I still deserve that grace?"

⮑ "What if I mess up again?"

⮑ "What if they say they've released it, but it comes back later?"

You may also feel impatient:

⮑ "Why aren't we past this yet?"

⮑ "I've apologized so many times — what more can I do?"

Remember: resentment grew over time because safety was missing over time. It will release over time as safety is rebuilt over time.

Your role in this step is not to **push** for release. Your role is to **keep showing up in a way that makes release possible**:

⮑ staying grounded when the hurt is named again

⮩ continuing to take responsibility when needed

⮩ being patient with the rhythm of their nervous system

When you say, "I don't need you to be over this on my timetable. I'll keep showing you I'm here," you become an ally of their release instead of an obstacle to it.

That is powerful.

You're now standing at one of the most tender parts of this whole process — the place where protection starts to loosen and space for healing begins to open.

The next page, **Worksheet 4: Release the Resentment**, is designed **for the partner who was hurt**. It's not about forcing forgiveness or pretending you're "over it." It's simply a guided space to notice what you're still carrying, what feels even *slightly* safer to loosen, and what you still need in order to keep softening.

If you're the partner who caused the hurt, your job in this step is to keep showing up steadily — to read, listen, and continue offering safety, not pressure.

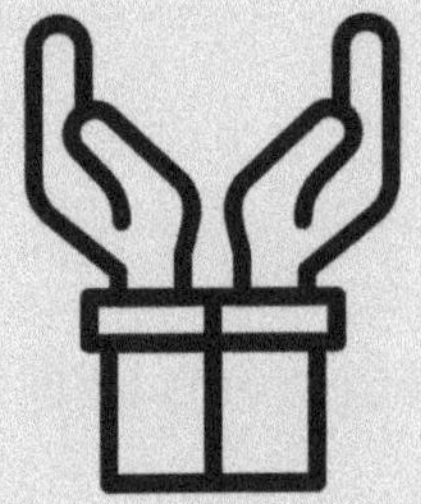

RELEASE THE RESENTMENT

Letting Go Without Rushing Yourself

Releasing resentment is an internal process — not excusing, not forgetting — loosening the grip of the story so your heart can breathe again.

Part 1: What the Resentment Is About

The resentment I feel is about:

Part 2: How Resentment Protects Me

Resentment often functions as armor. What is the resentment protecting you from?

Part 3: The Cost of Holding It

How does holding this resentment impact you, your body, or your relationship?

Part 4: Compassionate Reframe

What is a gentler, more spacious narrative you could begin to consider? E.g. *"Even though this hurt, I know my partner cares deeply for me and would not intentionally try to hurt me."*

Part 5: Resentment Release Statement

Complete the sentence:

"I am loosening my grip on this resentment by _______, so I can experience more _______."

Part 6: Softening Practices

What helps your heart soften?

- ⚪ Breathing
- ⚪ Journaling
- ⚪ Talking with partner
- ⚪ Movement
- ⚪ Prayer/meditation
- ⚪ Time
- ⚪ Other: ____

Which one will you practice this week?

Part 7: Gentle Check-In

What feels different in your body after naming all of this?

What This Step Makes Possible

When resentment releases, even a little:

- ⤵ connection becomes easier
- ⤵ playfulness returns
- ⤵ affection feels more natural
- ⤵ the body relaxes in each other's presence
- ⤵ trust grows
- ⤵ the story of the relationship shifts toward hope

Resentment is a prison.
Release is the key.

You don't need perfection.
You only need movement.

Releasing resentment creates the space where repair can finally take root.

Resentment keeps the heart guarded, the body tense, and the mind rehearsing old stories for protection. Letting go — even a little — signals that the nervous system feels safer, more open, and more willing to re-engage.

But release is not the same as repair. Release clears the emotional debris so the path forward becomes visible.

What happens next determines whether the relationship simply stops hurting…
or begins to heal.

Release softens the heart.
Repair strengthens the bond.

Release says, "I'm no longer holding this against you."
Repair says, "Let's build something better together."

Without release, repair feels forced.
Without repair, release has nowhere to land.

This is why the HEART Model™ ends with turning toward each other — not as a performance or duty, but as a shared, hopeful movement into a more secure future.

You've honored the hurt.
You've empathized with the experience.

You've acknowledged the impact.
You've loosened resentment's grip.

And now, with clarity, safety, and openness in place, you're ready for the final step: **Turn Toward Repair**

06

TURN TOWARD REPAIR

█ Choosing Connection Again — One Small Turn at a Time

Turning toward repair is the culmination of The HEART Model™. It's the moment when partners shift from processing the hurt to actively rebuilding connection. This is where the work becomes embodied — where intentions turn into action and where the relationship regains its sense of steadiness and hope.

Repair does not mean the hurt is erased.
Repair means the relationship is re-engaged.

> *Repair does not mean the hurt is erased. Repair means the relationship is re-engaged.*

You do not need to have everything figured out to take this step.
You don't need the perfect words.
You don't need a flawless plan.

You only need the willingness to turn toward your partner instead of away.

Every relationship rises or falls on these small moments.

John Gottman's research calls them "bids for connection," and they are the heartbeat of relational resilience. When a relationship is hurting, turning toward repair becomes a conscious, intentional version of the same practice.

Not dramatic.
Not grand.
Just deliberate.

Why This Step Matters

Once hurt has been expressed, understood, acknowledged, and softened, the relationship is open — but not yet reconnected. Without the final step, couples may leave a conversation feeling calm but not close, peaceful but not bonded.

Turning toward repair bridges the gap.

This step:

➲ rebuilds trust through consistent behavior

➲ creates new emotional memory to replace the painful one

➲ strengthens attachment through responsiveness

➲ prevents lingering distance

➲ builds a forward-focused path

➲ reinforces that the relationship is capable of healing

It is not a performance.
It is not pressure.
It is not forced forgiveness.

It is choosing connection again.

From an attachment and nervous system lens, repair teaches both bodies, *"We know how to find each other after a rupture."* That embodied memory is what makes the relationship feel safer over time — not because you never hurt each other, but because you now know how to come back.

Sofia and David

Finding their way back to each other.

After Sofia felt the beginnings of release, the energy in the room shifted. You could feel it. Something softened between them, like the tension that had been stretching the space finally let go.

David turned toward her — literally. He angled his body toward hers, placed his phone face down on the coffee table, and reached out his hand.

"I want to do this differently moving forward," he said.
"When you're sharing something vulnerable, I want to slow down and actually be with you. You matter too much for me to stay distracted."

Sofia nodded, tears rising — not from hurt now, but from relief.

"I want that too," she said softly. "And I'll try to tell you sooner when I'm feeling sensitive instead of hoping you'll just know."

There it was.
Two tiny turns toward each other.
Two small commitments.
Two nervous systems saying, "We're still in this."

Repair is rarely loud.
Repair is rarely dramatic.

Repair is quiet, intentional, relational.

What Turning Toward Repair Actually Looks Like

Turning toward repair can take countless forms:

- clarifying a need moving forward
- making a small behavioral shift
- creating an agreement to revisit something
- checking in later that day
- offering a moment of affection
- following through on something meaningful
- increasing presence and attentiveness
- adjusting a pattern that contributed to the hurt

Examples of repair moves include:

- "Next time, I'll pause and make eye contact before responding."
- "Can we sit together tonight and reconnect for 10 minutes?"
- "Would a hug feel good right now?"
- "I want to support you — how can I do that today?"
- "This matters to me. Want to talk again tomorrow and make a plan?"

Repair is *relational creativity.*
It's designing small, steady actions that rebuild emotional trust.

> *Repair is relational creativity.*

Why Repair Must Be Small to Be Effective

Couples often try to repair with big promises:

- "I'll never do that again."
- "I'll change everything."
- "I'll be better."

But relationships don't heal through sweeping vows.
They heal through tiny turns toward each other.

> Relationships don't heal through sweeping vows.
> They heal through tiny turns toward each other.

Tiny turns are the small, consistent choices you make:

- to pause instead of react
- to listen instead of defend
- to reach instead of retreat
- to check in instead of assume
- to soften instead of escalate

Each turn is small, but over time they accumulate — rewiring the emotional rhythm of the relationship.

Tiny turns work because they are:

- doable
- sustainable
- gentle
- predictable
- calming to the nervous system

They don't overwhelm.
They don't require perfection.
They build safety a few inches at a time.

Turning toward repair is the intentional practice of making these tiny turns again and again.

The Internal Shift Behind Repair

To turn toward repair, something inside must shift from **protection** to **connection**.

It does not mean agreeing with everything, or erasing your own needs, or "being the bigger person."

It means asking: *"What would it look like for me to move toward you right now?"*

That is the birthplace of reconnection.

Often this shift is felt in the body first:

- jaw unclenching
- shoulders lowering
- breath deepening
- a tiny softening in the chest

Your body is saying, *"We don't have to armor up in this moment. We can reach instead."*

The Science Behind Repair

Relational neuroscience shows that when partners consistently turn toward each other:

- oxytocin increases
- threat responses decrease
- emotional co-regulation strengthens
- trust becomes embodied, not just intellectual
- the negative cycle loses traction
- the relationship becomes more resilient
- the heart recovers faster from future hurts

Turning toward repair creates new emotional memory.

Your nervous system literally learns, *"We know how to come back together."*

Continuing Sofia and David's Story

After their moment of connection, the room felt different.

Sofia exhaled fully for the first time in days.
David's shoulders were no longer tense.

Repair had begun.

Later that week, David intentionally set his phone aside when Sofia started talking. She noticed. And just as importantly, she responded — with warmth, with gratitude, with ease. Their dynamic didn't transform in a single night, but it shifted.

A tiny turn.
Then another.
Then another.

This is repair.

Not forgetting.
Not pretending.

But gently rebuilding.

Turning toward repair creates new emotional memory.

For the One Who Was Hurt

If you're the partner who was hurt, turning toward repair can feel both hopeful and risky.

Part of you may think:

➲ "What if I lean in and they go back to the old pattern?"

➲ "If I soften, will I lose the protection I've had?"

➲ "Do I trust these changes yet?"

Repair does not ask you to ignore your instincts. It invites you to listen to **all** of them:

➲ the part that is still cautious,

➲ the part that is tired,

⮑ and the part that quietly longs to feel close again.

You are allowed to move slowly.

Turning toward repair might look like:

⮑ agreeing to a small new ritual (a nightly check-in, a weekly walk)

⮑ saying "thank you" when you notice a change, even if you're still watchful

⮑ letting yourself enjoy a moment of connection without interrogating it

You don't have to fling the doors wide open. You can crack the door and see if consistency shows up.

Your willingness to participate in repair is a gift — not just to your partner, but to your own heart. It gives you a chance to experience a relationship where your pain is taken seriously *and* your longing for closeness is honored.

For the One Who Hurt

If you're the partner who caused the injury, turning toward repair is where your empathy and responsibility take on a daily, lived shape.

You might feel pressure:

⮑ "I have to be perfect now."

⮑ "If I slip even once, everything will be ruined."

⮑ "If they're still sensitive, I must be failing."

Repair is not about flawless performance. It's about **reliable effort**.

Repair is not about flawless performance. It's about reliable effort.

Your repair moves might look like:

⮑ following through on what you said you'd do

⮑ checking in gently: "How is this feeling for you lately?"

⮑ being open if your partner says, "I'm still a little tender there"

⮑ staying regulated when old pain gets touched again

You can say:

⮑ "I know this isn't fixed overnight, but I'm committed to showing up differently."

⮌ "If you feel wobbly about trusting this, that makes sense. I'll keep showing you."

Turning toward repair is your chance to live in alignment with the partner you want to be — not to erase the past, but to create a different pattern for the future.

Let's move to our final worksheet: Turn Toward Repair

Reconnection & Action Planning Sheet: *(To be completed by both partners.)*

Repair is not a moment — it is a movement. This worksheet helps you identify the next small, meaningful step.

Part 1: What Needs Repair

What specific moment or pattern is asking for attention?

Part 2: Your Hope for This Repair

What outcome or emotional shift do you hope for?

Part 3: A Small, Doable Step

What is one immediate step you can take to move toward reconnection?

Part 4: What You Can Offer

What gesture, conversation, boundary, or practice would help healing begin?

Part 5: What You Need From Your Partner

What would help *you* feel safer, softer, or more open?

Part 6: Repair Agreement

Complete the sentence:

"This week, we will move toward each other by ______________________________________

and support that movement by ____."

Part 7: Gentle Check-In

What feels hopeful as you imagine this repair?

When partners turn toward repair:

➲ tenderness returns

➲ emotional safety deepens

➲ the distance closes

➲ trust rebuilds

➲ the relationship gains momentum

➲ future hurts feel less threatening

➲ connection becomes easier to access

Repair is the emotional equivalent of coming home.

It doesn't mean you'll never have another rupture. It means that when ruptures come, you have a map — and the confidence that you can find your way back

Repair is where the relationship begins to feel like itself again — softened, supported, and steady.

But even repair is not the finish line.
It is the beginning of a new pattern, a new posture, a new way of moving toward each other with intention.

Turning toward repair doesn't erase what happened.
It creates a future that's no longer defined by it.

> Turning toward repair doesn't erase what happened. It creates a future that's no longer defined by it.

When partners make small, consistent repair moves, the relationship gains a new kind of rhythm:

➲ one where reaching out feels safer,

➲ where honesty lands softer,

➲ where the next hard moment doesn't feel like a threat to the bond.

Repair also reveals something deeper: that healing is not a single act, and closeness is not a one-time decision. It's a practice — a way of being with each other.

This is why the HEART Model ends with repair but the relationship doesn't.

Repair becomes a lifestyle.
A posture.
A commitment to keep turning toward each other, even when old patterns try to pull you apart.

The work doesn't stop here.
It continues in conversations over dinner, in apologies whispered in the hallway, in the choice to soften when you could protect, and in the courage to speak when silence feels safer.

Repair is the place where love becomes mature.
Resilient.
Rooted.

As Sofia and David discovered, the tiniest turns have the power to redirect the entire trajectory of a relationship. And the same is possible for you.

With the HEART Model, you now have a clear, compassionate path for moving through hurt and into healing.

The conclusion will help you consolidate this journey, integrate what you've learned, and carry these practices into the everyday moments that shape your relationship the most.

Let's bring it all together.

CONCLUSION

Healing in a relationship does not happen all at once.
It happens in moments — small, human, ordinary moments where two partners choose connection over distance and presence over protection.

The HEART Model™ gives you a pathway for those moments, a rhythm that helps you navigate emotional injuries with clarity, compassion, and courage. But HEART is not just a sequence of steps. It is a posture — a way of moving through your relationship with intention.

People sometimes imagine that healthy couples don't hurt each other. But the truth is far more hopeful: healthy couples repair well. They move through hurt with honesty. They soften where they once would have hardened. They turn toward each other when they once might have turned away.

Healthy couples repair well.

You've now walked through the five movements that make repair possible:

- ⮑ **Honor the Hurt** — naming what happened and how it impacted you.
- ⮑ **Empathize with the Experience** — staying open enough to understand each other's inner world.
- ⮑ **Acknowledge Responsibility** — owning your part without collapsing into shame.
- ⮑ **Release the Resentment** — loosening what no longer protects you.
- ⮑ **Turn Toward Repair** — choosing connection again, one tiny turn at a time.

Taken together, these movements rewrite the emotional pattern of the relationship. They transform the way you navigate conflict, misunderstandings, and tender moments. They help you build something deeper than harmony: **emotional safety**.

With emotional safety, couples don't grow apart — they grow forward.
They don't fear conflict — they use it.
They don't avoid vulnerability — they welcome it.
They don't hide their hearts — they offer them.

From an attachment and nervous system perspective, HEART is how you slowly build a secure base with each other. Each time you move through these steps, your bodies learn:

"We can survive hard moments."
"We can come back together."
"We are not alone in this."

Over time, that memory settles into your bones.

When It Isn't Perfect (Because It Won't Be)

The power of HEART is not in its perfection, but in its practice.

You will not move through these steps flawlessly.
No couple does.

Some days you'll move through all five.
Other days, you'll only manage one.

Sometimes you'll get stuck.
Sometimes you'll circle back.
Sometimes you'll forget the model entirely.

And that's okay.

The goal was never perfection.
The goal is **movement**.

Every time you honor hurt, you disrupt old emotional patterns.
Every time you offer empathy, you soften the cycle.
Every time you take responsibility, you build trust.
Every time you release resentment, you create space for connection.
Every time you turn toward repair, you create a new emotional memory — one that tells your relationship, *"We know how to find our way back."*

Healing is not linear, and repair is not a finish line.
Repair is a rhythm — an ongoing, gentle practice of turning toward each other in the moments that matter most.

A Word to Each of You

If you are the one who has carried the hurt, I want you to know this:

Your pain makes sense.
Your longing for safety is not too much.

You are allowed to move at the pace your body can handle, to ask for what you need more than once, to feel cautious and hopeful at the same time. Using HEART is not about talking yourself out of what happened. It's about letting your story be met with care, so your heart no longer has to protect you all by itself.

If you are the one who caused the injury, I want you to hear this:

Your willingness to stay present is part of the repair.
Your courage to own your impact matters more than getting it perfect.
Your growth is not erased by the worst thing you've done.

You are allowed to feel shame and still choose responsibility, to feel scared and still stay in the room, to believe you are more than this moment and act like it. Using HEART does not mean living forever in apology. It means becoming a partner who can face the truth, care about the impact, and keep showing up differently over time.

Carrying HEART into Everyday Life

You may use this model in big conversations around major injuries, but the real transformation happens when HEART sneaks into the small moments:

- pausing to notice hurt instead of brushing it off,
- saying, "You make sense," instead of, "You're overreacting,"
- offering a simple, "I see how that landed. I'm sorry,"
- choosing to soften a little sooner,
- reaching out a little more often.

If you keep showing up to that practice, quietly and consistently, your relationship will grow stronger, softer, and more secure than you ever imagined.

Wherever you are as you close this book — raw from recent hurt, cautiously hopeful, or simply wanting to stay connected over the long haul — you do not have to do it perfectly. You only have to keep turning toward each other.

Your heart knows the way.
Your partner's heart does too.

Now you have the steps.

And every time you choose to practice them, you're not just repairing a moment — you're building a relationship where love is not only felt, but *lived*.

FREQUENTLY ASKED QUESTIONS

1. What if only one of us wants to do this model?

That's okay — HEART can begin with just one partner.

Repair in relationships often starts with the person who is most willing. When one partner shows up with honesty, empathy, and responsibility, it softens the system and often invites the other to engage.

If you found this workbook on your own and want to work on forgiveness, start by asking a simple question:

"What role did I play in this hurt?"

Then begin where that truth leads you:

- **If you were the one who was hurt**
  Your work begins with **Honor the Hurt**.
  Start by naming what happened, how it impacted you, and what it stirred up inside. You can walk through that step on your own first, then *invite* your partner into the process by sharing your Impact Statement or worksheet — not as a demand, but as an honest window into your experience.

- **If you were the one who caused the hurt**
  Your work will most naturally begin with **Empathize with the Experience** and **Acknowledge Responsibility**.
  Start by imagining what the moment felt like for your partner, then move into owning your part without excuses, blame-shifting, or collapse.

Even if your partner isn't ready (or willing) to walk through every step with you, your side of the work still matters. HEART is a five-step model, but it rarely unfolds in a straight line. It often begins with one person taking one brave step — and letting the rest emerge over time.

2. Can HEART work if the hurt is big?

Yes — but slowly.
HEART is not designed to rush forgiveness or minimize deep pain. For major injuries (affairs, betrayals, long-standing patterns), you may need therapy or coaching to walk through these steps with support. The model still applies, but the pacing must be gentler, and safety must be rebuilt layer by layer.

3. What if the resentment comes back after we've released it?

That's normal. Resentment is like scar tissue — it loosens over time, not all at once. If it returns, it doesn't mean you failed. It just means another layer needs empathy, clarity, or reassurance. Revisit the step you need. HEART is designed to cycle as many times as needed.

4. Do we have to move through all five steps in order every time?

No. HEART has a natural flow, but real relationships are not linear. Sometimes you'll start with empathy, or acknowledgment, or even repair. The model is there to guide you, not to trap you in a sequence. Use it in whatever way best supports safety and connection in the moment.

5. What if one partner gets defensive or shuts down?

Pause. Don't push through. Defensiveness or withdrawal usually means the nervous system is overwhelmed. Stop the conversation, take a break, regulate, and return when both bodies feel grounded. HEART works best when both partners feel emotionally available.

6. Can we use this model without a therapist?

Absolutely. Many couples use HEART on their own — the steps are simple, accessible, and relational. If you ever feel stuck, you can bring the model into therapy or coaching as a shared framework. It often accelerates the work because you both have a shared language.

7. How often should we use HEART?

As often as needed. Use it for big hurts, small ruptures, moments of disconnect, or any time something feels "off." Over time, HEART becomes a natural rhythm — the way you approach tension, repair, and connection.

8. What if we have different memories of what happened?

That's completely normal. You don't need identical memories to move toward healing. HEART focuses on the **impact**, not the exact details. Two truths can exist side by side, and both can be honored without forcing agreement.

9. What if we're still angry when we start?

Then start with regulation. HEART is not designed for dysregulated moments. Take space. Breathe. Ground. Come back when your body is ready. A regulated conversation is far more effective than a fast one.

10. Are we supposed to forgive at the end of this?

No. Forgiveness is never forced, expected, or required. HEART creates the environment where forgiveness could eventually happen, but the goal is **connection** and **understanding**, not forced absolution. Go at a pace that honors your heart.

11. What if we try this and it doesn't work right away?

That is still progress. HEART changes patterns over time, not overnight. Every conversation, every softening, every tiny turn toward each other is a win. Keep practicing. Small shifts compound.

12. Who is the HEART Model™ for?

HEART is for couples who:

➲ want to communicate more clearly

➲ want to understand each other's emotions

➲ want to repair conflict more effectively

➲ want to build emotional safety

➲ want to deepen intimacy

➲ want a simple, practical model they can use anytime

It's not about being perfect — it's about being willing.

13. How do we use the worksheets in the back of the workbook?

Because The HEART Model™ is created for couples, each appendix has a specific purpose:

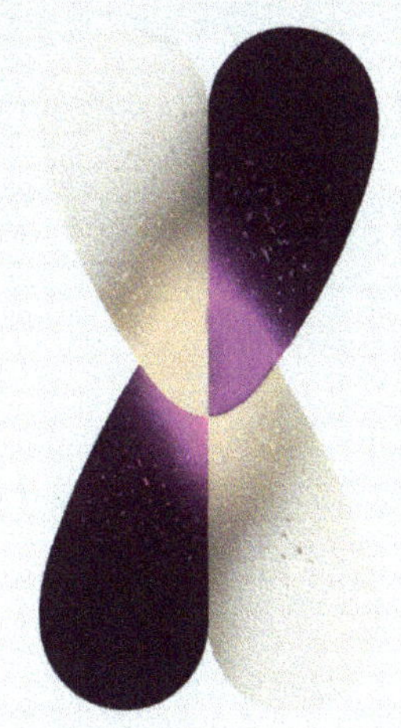

HEART WORKSHEETS

⮑ **Honor the Hurt** is for the one who was hurt.

⮑ **Empathize with the Experience** is for the partner who created the hurt.

⮑ **Acknowledge Responsibility** is also for the one who created the hurt.

⮑ **Release the Resentment** is for the partner who was hurt.

⮑ **Turn Toward Repair** is for both partners.

APPENDIX B - F

The EMPATHY MAP is to be used whenever one partner needs assistance on how to access empathy. This is a worksheet to use as often as needed.

The HEART Cycle Wheel is a visual representation of the repair process. It shows the natural, relational movement from hurt → understanding → accountability → softening → reconnection. Instead of seeing repair as a straight line, the wheel helps couples understand it as a circular rhythm — one they can return to as many times as needed. This model emphasizes that repair is not something you do once but something you practice whenever disconnection happens. Every moment of hurt becomes an opportunity to move through the cycle and find each other again.

USING HEART IN REAL TIME CONFLICTS

The HEART Model™ was designed not just for reflection after the fact, but also for real time use — in the middle of misunderstandings, hurt feelings, or moments of disconnect. This appendix gives couples a step-by-step way to move through conflict without spiraling into the negative cycle. It keeps things grounded, slow, and emotionally safe. Think of this as a "first response kit" for your relationship.

The **QUICK-START GUIDE** is your "start here" page — perfect for moments when you feel off, misunderstood, tense, or unsure how to reconnect. Use it when you don't have the time or emotional bandwidth to walk through the full chapters. This is HEART in its simplest, most accessible form.

PROMPTS AND SCRIPTS is a simple way to use the HEART Model™ anytime you feel disconnected. These prompts and scripts are not meant to be repeated verbatim — they're scaffolding. Use them as starting points to help you access connection when your mind or emotions feel scrambled. Sometimes the hardest part of repair is knowing where to begin. These phrases give couples an emotionally safe starting point.

EMPATHY MAP WORKSHEET

EMPATHY MAP WORKSHEET

Seeing the moment through your partner's eyes — without needing to agree.

Empathy is the bridge that softens defensiveness, deepens understanding, and opens the door to repair. Use this worksheet anytime you want to slow down and understand your partner's inner experience more fully.

This exercise works best when done with curiosity, not pressure — and with imagination, not certainty. You are not trying to "guess right." You are simply trying to *understand generously.*

1. What were they feeling in that moment?

(Examples: overwhelmed, afraid, embarrassed, lonely, pressured, misunderstood)

2. What might they have been *afraid* of or protecting?

(Note: Even anger is often a cover for fear or vulnerability.)

3. What were they *needing* but unable to express?

(Examples: reassurance, understanding, space, closeness, clarity, comfort)

4. What might have been happening in their nervous system?

Were they:

- ○ overwhelmed?
- ○ shutting down?
- ○ bracing?
- ○ trying to manage emotion?
- ○ scanning for safety?

5. What personal history or trigger could have been activated?

(You don't have to know for sure — just explore the possibility.)

6. What story might they have been telling themselves?

(Examples: "I'm failing," "I can't get this right," "I'm not important," "I'm being blamed.")

7. If I place myself in their shoes, I imagine they might say:

8. Something I understand differently now is:

9. My empathy statement:

Try completing on of these or write your own in the space below.

- "I can see how that moment felt _______________________________ for you."

- "I didn't understand before, but now I see how this impacted you."

- "It makes sense to me that you would feel _______________ given what happened."

- "I get why that landed painfully — I'm here with you."

10. What I want to hold with tenderness moving forward:

This worksheet can be used:

- ✓ before a repair conversation
- ✓ when one partner is struggling
- ✓ as a daily or weekly check-in
- ✓ after a conflict
- ✓ when communication feels stuck
- ✓ in therapy, coaching, or pastoral settings

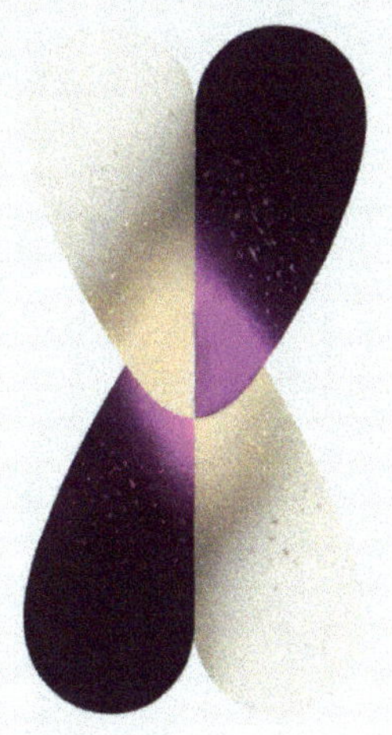

THE HEART CYCLE WHEEL

A clear, visual map of how couples move from hurt back into connection.

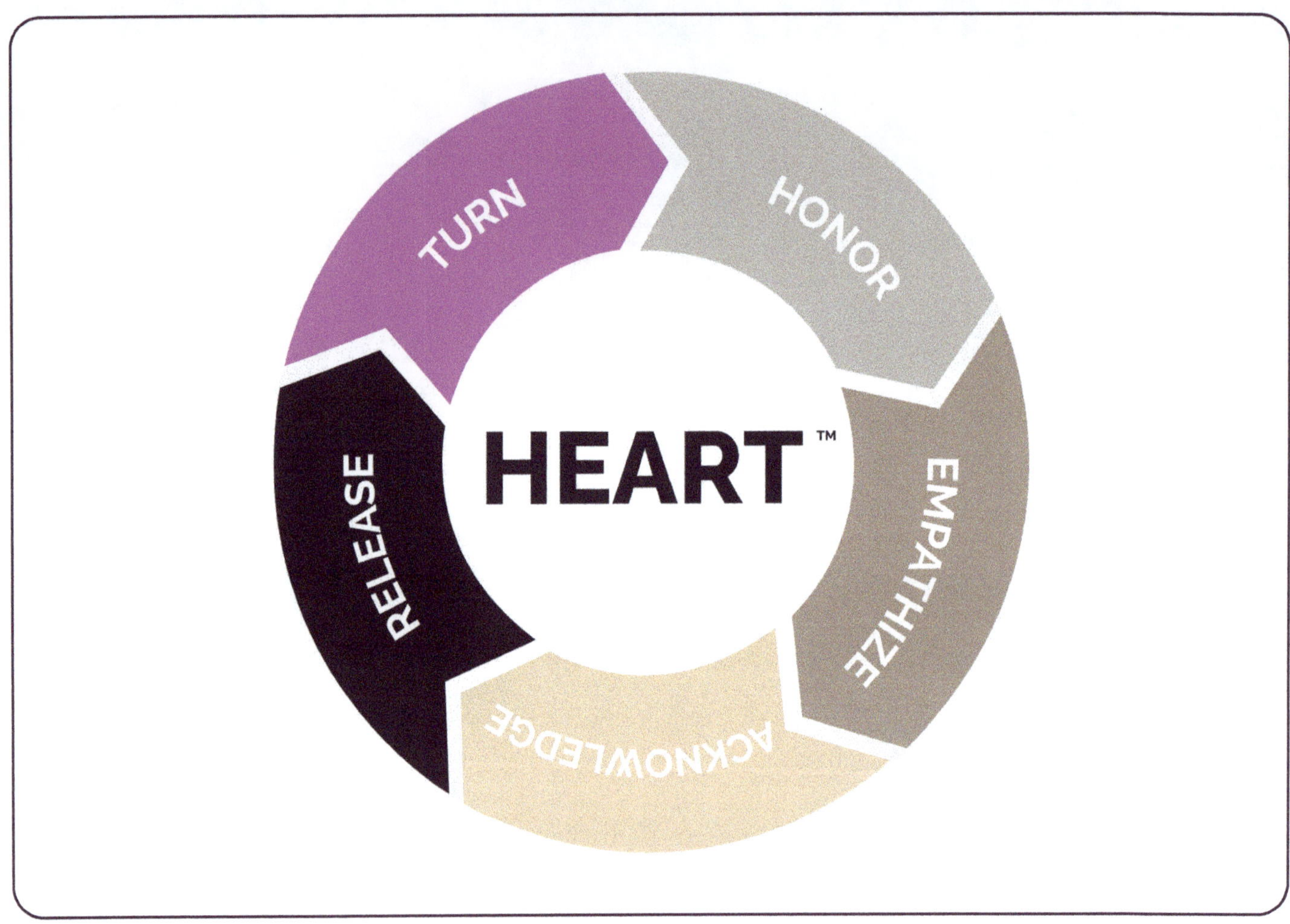

The HEART Cycle Wheel is a visual representation of the repair process. It shows the natural, relational movement from hurt → understanding → accountability → softening → reconnection.

Instead of seeing repair as a straight line, the wheel helps couples understand it as a **circular rhythm** — one they can return to as many times as needed.

This model emphasizes that repair is not something you do once but something you practice *whenever disconnection happens.* Every moment of hurt becomes an opportunity to move through the cycle and find each other again.

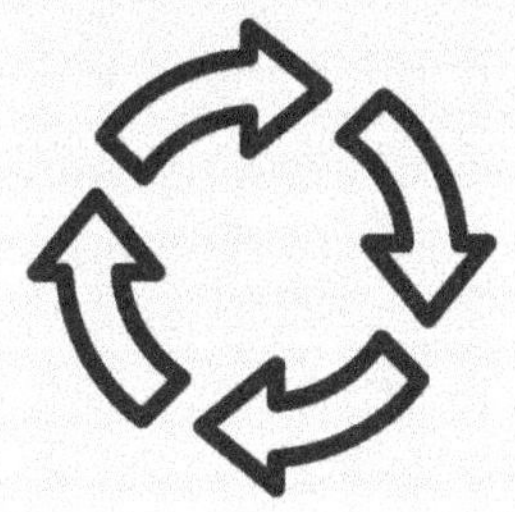# THE HEART CYCLE WHEEL

1. Hurt → Honor

Every repair begins with a moment of hurt — big or small.
The first step is bringing that hurt into the light with clarity and honesty.

Honor the Hurt means:	✔ naming the moment ✔ naming the emotion ✔ naming the meaning beneath it

It's the doorway to connection.

2. Honor → Empathize

Once a hurt is named, the next movement is into empathy.
This is where each partner tries to understand the emotional undercurrent of the moment
— their own and each other's.

Empathize with the Experience means:	✔ imagining the partner's emotional world ✔ staying curious ✔ softening defensiveness ✔ slowing down your nervous system

Connection begins here.

3. Empathize → Acknowledge

With empathy established, both partners can more easily see their part in how things unfolded.

Acknowledge Responsibility means:
- owning impact without shame
- recognizing what your partner needed
- understanding how your behavior landed
- offering an authentic apology

This is where emotional safety begins to rebuild.

4. Acknowledge → Release

As responsibility is acknowledged, the partner who was hurt often feels safer — and safety is what allows resentment to loosen.

Release the Resentment means:
- softening
- loosening your grip
- letting go of what no longer protects you
- releasing the emotional "replay"

Release is not a moment; it's a gentle unwinding.

5. Release → Turn Toward Repair

When resentment softens, connection becomes possible again.

<table>
<tr>
<td>Turn Toward Repair means:</td>
<td>

✔ taking a tiny turn toward your partner

✔ making a small behavioral shift

✔ offering reassurance or closeness

✔ reconnecting emotionally or physically

✔ rebuilding the sense of "us"

</td>
</tr>
</table>

This is not a grand gesture — it's a consistent rhythm.

6. Repair → Connection

The final movement of the wheel is the restored sense of connection that comes through repair.

<table>
<tr>
<td>Connection looks like:</td>
<td>

✔ warmth returning

✔ shoulders softening

✔ tenderness resurfacing

✔ a sense of "we're okay"

✔ emotional safety deepening

</td>
</tr>
</table>

Connection isn't the end of the wheel.
It's the *renewed starting point* for future moments of repair.

Why a Wheel?

Because repair is *cyclical.*
You will return to these steps again and again in your relationship — not because you're failing but because you're human.

The wheel communicates:	✓ repair is always available ✓ no step is final ✓ you can re-enter anywhere ✓ the model is flexible ✓ there is always a path back to each other

It turns the idea of forgiveness from a pressure point into a practice.

How Couples Should Use the Wheel

You can use the HEART Cycle Wheel:	✓ during conflict, to orient yourselves ✓ after conflict, to debrief what happened ✓ at calm times, to understand your patterns ✓ in therapy, coaching, or couples groups ✓ in intensives or marriage conferences ✓ as daily or weekly check-ins

It helps partners ask:	✓ "Where are we in the wheel right now?" ✓ "What step would help us move forward?" ✓ "What small turn could help us stay connected?"

This transforms conflict from chaotic to structured — without feeling clinical or rigid.

USING HEART IN REAL-TIME CONFLICTS

A simple, steady way to stay connected when emotions rise.

The HEART Model™ was designed not just for reflection after the fact, but also for **real-time use** — in the middle of misunderstandings, hurt feelings, or moments of disconnect.

This appendix gives couples a step-by-step way to move through conflict without spiraling into the negative cycle. It keeps things grounded, slow, and emotionally safe.

Think of this as a "first response kit" for your relationship.

1. Start With the Body, Not the Words

Real-time repair begins with regulation.

If either partner is:

- flooded
- defensive
- shut down
- overwhelmed
- angry
- numb
- panicked

then **pause the conversation.**

Say:

- "Give me a second — I want to stay connected."
- "I need a breath so I can hear you better."
- "Let's slow down for a moment."

Tiny regulation = massive relational protection.
(You don't need to relax — you just need to *ground*.)

2. Use the HEART Check-In

Before diving into the steps, do a 30-second micro check-in:

H	Am I hurt? What's the emotion?
E	Can I imagine their internal world right now?
A	Is there anything I can own already?
R	Is resentment rising?
T	What would turning toward look like in this moment?

You do *not* need to move through all five steps — the check-in simply orients you.

3. Slow the Moment With a "Connection Phrase"

These phrases interrupt the negative cycle and re-engage the bond:

- ✔ "I'm here. Let's slow down."
- ✔ "I want to understand you."
- ✔ "We're on the same team."
- ✔ "I'm trying to stay close while we talk."
- ✔ "This matters to me."

You're not fixing — you're staying connected.

4. Use HEART in Mini-Form (The 30-Second Version)

When conflict is happening *in real time*, you won't say paragraphs. You'll say **micro-steps**.

Here's the real-time version:

▶ **Honor (10 seconds)**
"I'm feeling hurt because ____________."

▶ **Empathize (10 seconds)**
"I can imagine you might be feeling ____________."

▶ **Acknowledge (5 seconds)**
"I can see how my reaction impacted you."

▶ **Release (moment)**
Take one slow breath.
"This isn't me against you."

▶ **Turn Toward (5–10 seconds)**
"What's one small way we can reconnect right now?"

That's it. Simple. Fast. Regulating.

5. Use "Tiny Turns" to Interrupt Escalation

Conflict escalates when partners move away.

Repair begins when partners make **tiny turns toward each other**, such as:

- softening your tone
- uncrossing your arms
- sitting beside instead of across
- making gentler eye contact
- reaching out a hand
- saying "I'm listening"
- pausing instead of reacting

These micro-movements shift the nervous system from threat → safety.

6. If One Partner is Flooded, Pause Without Punishment

Pausing is not abandonment — it's regulation.

Say:
- "I need a few minutes to settle. I'm coming back."
- "I want to keep talking, just not from this state."
- "Let's regroup in 10 minutes."

Scheduled returns calm anxiety, build trust, and protect connection.

7. Use the HEART Cycle Wheel as a "Where Are We?" Map

**During conflict,
pause and identify:**

- Are we in Hurt?
- Are we in Empathy?
- Are we in Defensiveness (opposite of Acknowledge)?
- Are we in Resentment?
- Are we ready for Repair?

Naming where you are immediately calms the cycle.

8. If the Conflict Gets Stuck, Try One of These Pathways

▶ **Pathway A: Reset the Conversation**
"Can we start over slower?"

▶ **Pathway B: Shift Into Empathy**
"Help me understand what was happening for you."

▶ **Pathway C: Own Something Small**
"You're right that I got sharp there."

▶ **Pathway D: Ground the Connection**
"I want us to get through this together."

These micro-pathways keep the conversation from derailing.

9. End the Conflict With a Repair Moment

Every conflict should end with some version of:

- a small act of connection
- a hug or hand squeeze
- a breath together
- a kind word
- a short commitment ("I'll try X next time")
- a shared moment (sitting together, walking, touching)

This seals the cycle.

Even if the conflict isn't fully resolved, a repair moment prevents emotional distance from hardening.

10. If the Moment Is Too Big, Move to the Full HEART Process Later

Some moments require the full model with:

- worksheets
- a guided conversation
- slower pacing
- therapist involvement
- deeper empathy

Real-time HEART isn't about solving everything — it's about staying connected enough to return to repair when you're grounded.

QUICK-START GUIDE FOR COUPLES

A simple way to use the HEART Model™ anytime you feel disconnected.

This quick-start guide is your "start here" page — perfect for moments when you feel off, misunderstood, tense, or unsure how to reconnect.

Use it when you don't have the time or emotional bandwidth to walk through the full chapters. This is HEART in its simplest, most accessible form.

THE HEART MINI-MODEL

H — Honor the Hurt (1–2 sentences)

Say what hurt and why, gently and clearly.

Example:
"I felt lonely earlier when you walked away while I was talking."

E — Empathize With the Experience (1–2 sentences)

Imagine your partner's emotional world.

Example:
"I can see how you might have felt overwhelmed or distracted."

A — Acknowledge Responsibility (1 sentence)

Own the impact, even if it wasn't intentional.

Example:

"I see how my tone sounded sharp — that wasn't fair to you."

R — Release the Resentment (pause + breath)

Soften the emotional grip.

Do:

- breathe once slowly
- drop your shoulders
- imagine setting the moment down

Say, if you want:

"I don't want this moment to harden between us."

T — Turn Toward Repair (1 tiny turn)

Make one small move toward connection.

Examples:

- "Can we try that moment again, slower?"
- "I want to feel close — can I sit next to you?"
- "What small shift can we make for next time?"
- "Can we hug?"

Tiny turns rebuild trust.

WHEN TO USE THIS QUICK-START GUIDE

Use this page when:

- something small stings
- emotions start rising
- you want to reconnect quickly
- you feel distance building
- resentment is whispering
- you don't have time for a deep conversation
- you want a structured way to avoid escalation

This is HEART "lite" — a compassionate shortcut.

REAL-LIFE EXAMPLE (Short & Simple)

▶ **Partner A:**
"I'm feeling hurt that you didn't respond when I asked for help earlier."

▶ **Partner B:**
"I can see how that felt dismissive. I was overloaded and didn't register it."

▶ **Partner A:**
"Thanks for owning that. I'm going to let go of holding onto that moment."

▶ **Partner B:**
"How about we reset? Want to take a walk together?"

Short. Clear. Connected.

PROMPTS & SCRIPTS FOR REPAIR

PROMPTS & SCRIPTS FOR REPAIR

A simple way to use the HEART Model™ anytime you feel disconnected.

These prompts and scripts are not meant to be repeated verbatim — they're scaffolding. Use them as starting points to help you access connection when your mind or emotions feel scrambled.

Sometimes the hardest part of repair is knowing where to begin. These phrases give couples an emotionally safe starting point.

1. HONOR THE HURT — Scripts for Naming Your Experience

Simple starters:

- "Something about that moment felt painful for me."
- "I felt hurt when ______."
- "I want to share what landed hard for me."
- "I'm not blaming you — I just want you to know what came up for me."

Deeper scripts:

- "I think what was underneath my reaction was feeling ______."
- "The meaning that moment held for me was ______."
- "I realized I felt ______ because I interpreted it as ______."

2. EMPATHIZE — Scripts for Seeing the Moment Through Their Eyes

Simple starters:

- ✔ "I can imagine that felt _______ for you."
- ✔ "I see why you reacted that way."
- ✔ "It makes sense you would feel _______ given what was happening."

Deeper scripts:

- ✔ "If I were in your shoes, I might have felt _______ too."
- ✔ "I didn't understand before, but I'm starting to see what that moment was like for you."
- ✔ "I think you might have been needing _______ and didn't know how to say it."

3. ACKNOWLEDGE — Scripts for Owning Your Part Without Collapse

Simple starters:

- ✔ "I see how my reaction impacted you."
- ✔ "I get that my tone came off sharper than I intended."
- ✔ "You're right — I wasn't fully present."

Deeper scripts:

- ✔ "I want to own my part: _______."
- ✔ "I didn't mean to, but I understand that my action caused _______."
- ✔ "I'm sorry for the impact that had on your heart."
- ✔ "Here's what I wish I had done instead: _______."

4. RELEASE — Scripts for Softening Resentment

(Release is gentle — not a delete button.)

Simple starters:

- "I want to let go of holding tight to this moment."
- "I'm ready to soften a little around this."
- "I'm trying to release the tension this brought up."

Deeper scripts:

- "A part of me still hurts, but another part of me wants to begin releasing this."
- "I don't want this to build a wall between us."
- "I'm choosing to loosen my grip on that moment."

For when you're not ready yet:

- "I'm not fully ready to release this, but I want to move toward it."
- "I need a little more time before I can soften here."

5. TURN TOWARD REPAIR — Scripts for Reconnection & Rebuilding

Simple starters:

- "Can we take a step toward each other right now?"
- "What's one small thing we can do differently moving forward?"
- "Can I sit next to you?"
- "Would a hug feel good?"

Deeper scripts:

- "A small turn I want to make is _______."
- "Here's something that would help me feel safe the next time something like this happens: _______."
- "How can we support each other better in moments like this?"
- "Let's reset. How do we want to move forward?"

6. WHEN THE MOMENT IS STUCK — Scripts for Getting Unstuck

To slow things down:

- "Can we pause? I want to stay connected."
- "Let's breathe for a second."
- "I'm overwhelmed — can we take a short break?"

To reset the tone:

- "I don't want this to become us vs. us."
- "We're on the same team."
- "I'm trying to work with you, not against you."

To clarify needs:

- "Here's what I need in this moment: ________."
- "What do you need right now?"
- "How can I support you in this conversation?"

7. CLOSING A REPAIR CONVERSATION — Scripts for Reconnection

To seal the moment:

- "Thank you for staying in this with me."
- "I feel closer to you after this."
- "We did good work just now."
- "I appreciate you."
- "I'm glad we're us."

ALSO BY MATT WADE, LMFT

Secure: 90 Days to a More Connected Relationship
Your daily guide to finding your way back to each other.

Secure is a 90-day guided journey for couples who feel stuck, distant, or ready to deepen their connection. Rooted in attachment science, real-life stories, and practical exercises, this workbook helps you identify your negative cycles, heal old wounds, and build emotional safety one day at a time. With simple prompts and structured practices, Secure gives you a clear, compassionate path back to closeness.

Secure is available on Amazon.

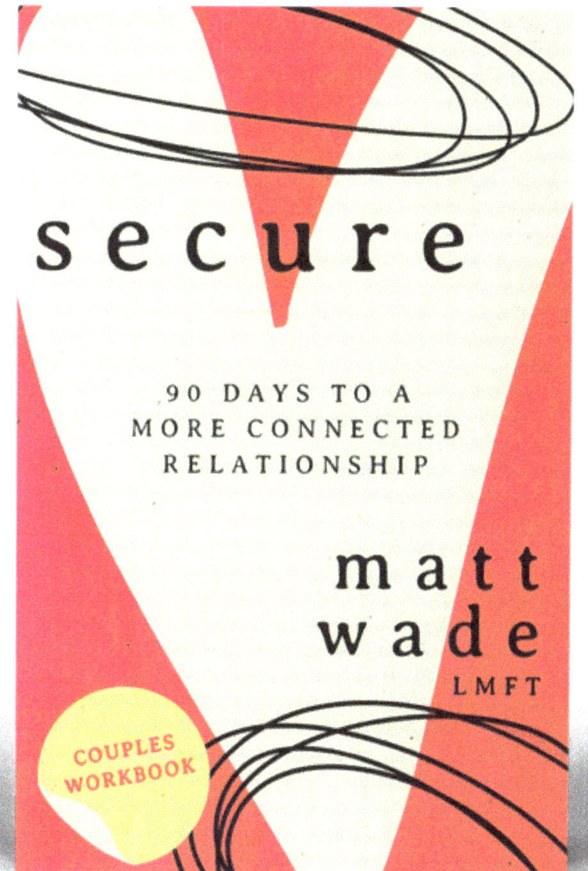

REFERENCES

Ainsworth, M. D. S., Blehar, M. C., Waters, E., & Wall, S. (1978). *Patterns of attachment: A psychological study of the strange situation*. Lawrence Erlbaum.

Baumeister, R. F., Stillwell, A. M., & Wotman, S. R. (1990). Victim and perpetrator accounts of interpersonal conflict: Autobiographical narratives about anger. *Journal of Personality and Social Psychology, 59*(5), 994–1005.

Bowlby, J. (1982). *Attachment and loss: Vol. 1. Attachment* (2nd ed.). Basic Books. (Original work published 1969)

Dana, D. (2018). *The polyvagal theory in therapy: Engaging the rhythm of regulation*. W. W. Norton.

Enright, R. D. (2012). *The forgiving life: A pathway to overcoming resentment and creating a legacy of love*. American Psychological Association.

Gottman, J. M., & Gottman, J. S. (1999). *The seven principles for making marriage work*. Crown.

Gottman, J. M., & DeClaire, J. (2001). *The relationship cure: A 5 step guide to strengthening your marriage, family, and friendships*. Crown.

Gottman, J. M., & Gottman, J. S. (2015). *10 principles for doing effective couples therapy*. W. W. Norton.

Hansen, M. J., Enright, R. D., Baskin, T. W., & Klatt, J. S. (2009). A palliative care intervention in forgiveness therapy for elderly terminally ill cancer patients. *Journal of Palliative Care, 25*(1), 51–60.

Johnson, S. M. (2008). *Hold me tight: Seven conversations for a lifetime of love*. Little, Brown.

Johnson, S. M. (2019). *Attachment theory in practice: Emotionally focused therapy (EFT) with individuals, couples, and families*. Guilford Press.

Lamott, A. (1999). *Traveling mercies: Some thoughts on faith*. Anchor Books.

McCullough, M. E., Pargament, K. I., & Thoresen, C. E. (2000). *Forgiveness: Theory, research, and practice.* Guilford Press.

Porges, S. W. (2011). *The polyvagal theory: Neurophysiological foundations of emotions, attachment, communication, and self-regulation.* W. W. Norton.

Siegel, D. J. (2010). *The developing mind: How relationships and the brain interact to shape who we are* (2nd ed.). Guilford Press.

Toussaint, L. L., Owen, A. D., & Cheadle, A. (2012). Forgive to live: Forgiveness, health, and longevity. *Journal of Behavioral Medicine, 35*(4), 375–386.

Worthington, E. L. (2006). *Forgiveness and reconciliation: Theory and application.* Routledge.